D0436921

A QUILT
FOR
CHRISTMAS

Center Point
Large Print

Also by Sandra Dallas and available from
Center Point Large Print:

True Sisters
Fallen Women

**This Large Print Book carries the
Seal of Approval of N.A.V.H.**

A QUILT
FOR
CHRISTMAS

SANDRA
DALLAS

CENTER POINT LARGE PRINT
THORNDIKE, MAINE

This Center Point Large Print edition is published
in the year 2014 by arrangement with St. Martin's Press.

Copyright © 2014 by Sandra Dallas.

The text of this Large Print edition is unabridged.
In other aspects, this book may vary from the original edition.
Printed in the United States of America on permanent paper.
Set in 16-point Times New Roman type.

ISBN: 978-1-62899-359-2

Library of Congress Cataloging-in-Publication Data

Dallas, Sandra.
  A quilt for Christmas / Sandra Dallas. — Center Point Large Print
edition.
  pages ; cm
  Summary: "Eliza Spooner makes her husband, Will, a special quilt to
keep him warm while serving in the Union army. Reaching out to help
others even after learning of Will's death, her greatest struggle will
come when a stranger returns the quilt"—Provided by publisher.
  ISBN 978-1-62899-359-2 (library binding : alk. paper)
  1. Quilting—Fiction. 2. Grief—Fiction. 3. Fugitive slaves—Fiction.
  4. Kansas—History—Civil War, 1861–1865—Fiction.
  5. Large type books. I. Title.
PS3554.A434Q55 2014b
813′.54—dc23
                                                              2014033223

For Danielle Egan-Miller
No writer ever had a better friend.

ACKNOWLEDGMENTS

Fallen Women, my last novel, was originally titled *Holladay Street*. Denver's red-light district was on Holladay Street, and the book, of course, is about nineteenth-century prostitution. My agent, Danielle Egan-Miller, read the title, however, and phoned to insist I change it. "Readers will think this is a Christmas book," she said. A few days later she phoned again. "Why don't you write a Christmas book?" she suggested. "Why don't you write a Christmas quilt book?"

Sure, I thought. About what? For me, coming up with a plot is the hardest thing about writing fiction. Not long after that, I had lunch with my dear friend Arnie Grossman. Arnie is a writer, too. He's also Jewish, and I doubt that he knows how to sew on a button. "Come up with a plot for a Christmas quilt book for me," I joked. He thought a moment and said, "What if a woman makes a quilt for her husband, a soldier in Iraq, as a Christmas present. He gets killed . . ." And there it was. Between us, we fleshed out the plot before coffee.

Of course, I didn't want to write about Iraq. I

don't care about computers and cell phones and automatic weapons. But I could write about the Civil War. I made other changes and refinements as I went along, but the basic plot remained. One addition was to make the characters in *A Quilt for Christmas* the grandmothers of those in *The Persian Pickle Club*. That idea tickled me, because I've always loved the Pickles, and readers often ask why I never wrote a sequel. Again, it's the difficulty of coming up with a plot.

So thank you, Arnie. And thanks to Danielle Egan-Miller for suggesting a Christmas quilt book, and to her associate, Joanna Mackenzie, and to Jennifer Enderlin, my St. Martin's editor, who always makes my writing better.

And thanks and Merry Christmas to my family—Bob, Dana, Kendal, Lloyd, and Forrest.

A QUILT
FOR
CHRISTMAS

PROLOGUE

November 20, 1864

It was a fine fall evening. The wind carried the smell of rotting apples and wood smoke and a hint of frost that would likely come after midnight. The setting sun made the stubble in the fields shimmer like flakes of mica and sent rays of light through the clouds as if the Almighty Himself were casting down the fiery shafts. Far off were the night sounds of cattle lowing, and nearer, of chickens clucking. The wind swirled papery dead leaves across the porch.

Usually, late November was the time of year when, the harvest done, the children asleep, Eliza would sit on the porch with her sewing, Will beside her, and they would talk of the day. They would tell of the chores done, the ones left for doing. Will would scan the sky for signs of the next day's weather, might say that his skin felt damp, which meant rain on the morrow. Often they sat without talking, were satisfied just to be there, together. Will was not a man to display his emotions, but sometimes he would reach for her hand, and Eliza would set her sewing aside, feeling his rough skin on her palm, and she was almost too happy to breathe. At those moments, her heart swelled, and she wondered why it was that she had been given such a good man, not always an easy man, but one who loved her. And she loved him. Oh yes.

"Well, Mrs. Spooner," he would say. "The Lord's give us a right nice life."

"The Lord and Will Spooner," she would reply. "My husband works harder than any man I know."

"Almost as hard as his wife," he would tell her.

Men were not given to such praise. Some of the men she was acquainted with were known to call their wives lazy or frivolous and to blame them for sloppy habits, were more likely to complain about meat cooked tough than compliment a pie made well. But not Will Spooner. He was a man to say what pleased him.

Eliza was not given to displays of affection, either, but she would squeeze her husband's hand, and he would press hers in return, and the message was as clear as if it had been written in a love letter: I am content. Theirs was not a perfect marriage—such a thing didn't exist—but it was as good a marriage as ever was.

Now, Eliza wiped her eyes with the back of her hand. The wind had blown up dust, she told herself, for she was not a woman to cry for sentiment.

The light was fading fast, but Eliza would not go inside, where it was too dark to sew. The house was a fine one, built sturdy of big logs and chinked so the air didn't blow through the cracks, but it had only a single window. If she were to sew inside, she would have to build up the fire to get enough light to see by, and that might awaken the children. Besides, she liked the outdoors, the smells and sounds and the chill of fall, although the cold made her fingers stiff, almost too stiff to hold a needle. She reached up to tighten her shawl and poked her finger through the fabric. The garment was old, had belonged to her mother and her grandmother before that, and it would have to be mended, not for the first time. It was now more mending than shawl, but there wasn't the money for a new one. There wasn't any money at all. Will hadn't thought about that when he left, hadn't thought she'd have to spend to have the wood chopped and be cheated at that. Eliza had had to scrimp to purchase the thread she sewed with and was quick to save the basting strands to be reused in the quilting.

Still, she was one of the lucky ones among the war widows, as the women whose men were away fighting for the Union called themselves. Her harvest was in, and there was enough to last through the winter if they were frugal. The potatoes were dug, the corn in the crib, the apples dried or pressed into cider. The costly woodpile was high, and the house snug. She was blessed, too, because there were no small children underfoot. Her two—Davy, fourteen, and Luzena, twelve—were old enough to be a help to her after their lessons at the table were done. Her son did the work of a man, while her daughter tended the house so that Eliza could work the fields with Davy. Together they had brought in the harvest as best they could, with much of it going to men who had helped on shares—and jayhawked her, she suspected. But at least there was enough to tide them over until the following year.

Eliza had everything she needed—except Will. But he would come back. Just a few months ago, in the late summer of 1864, he had gone for a soldier, a member of the Kansas Volunteers, to preserve the Union and free the slaves, but he would come back. He had promised. Until then, Eliza would manage.

Just as the sun sank below the horizon, Eliza bit off the last bit of thread, muttered, "Done," and held up the quilt for inspection. She was not given to self-praise, but she had to admit it was as fine a quilt as she had ever made, which meant it might be the finest in Wabaunsee County, Kansas. Eliza would not say she was the best quilter for miles around, but others would. She looked for imperfections but could not see them. Maybe that was not due to her fine sewing but because the dark had come on.

She had wanted to make the quilt with hearts and flowers to remind Will of the farm and let him know how much he was loved, but Eliza thought such a quilt might embarrass him among the soldiers. So she had chosen a Stars and Stripes quilt, one she had seen in *Peterson's Magazine*. The magazine was old, had been published in 1861, before the war began, and she hadn't seen it until the copy came around to her three years later. But the moment she saw it, she knew she had to make the quilt for Will. The magazine pattern was in color, hand-tinted with bright red and blue. The quilt was not exactly a flag, but inspired by the flag—a background of red and white stripes with a border of white stars on blue, and a star-filled blue triangle in the center. She hadn't made the quilt exactly like the pattern. What woman didn't want to bring her own creativity to a quilt? Besides, she'd wanted to make a small quilt, one that was the size of a hired man's comfort, because a full-size quilt would be large and too heavy for a bedroll. She knew the white would get dirty. Will had written that the soldiers slept on the ground, and when they found tents, the accommodations weren't clean. They sat on their blankets to eat and clean their guns, to read the Bible and play cards. But if the quilt were to be patterned after the Union flag, it had to have the white stripes.

With winter coming, Eliza had worried that

Will would take cold. The blankets issued to the soldiers, he had written, weren't much better than shoddy, sold to the War Department by a contractor who was more interested in profit than in providing warm bedding for the army. After reading the letter, Eliza knew she had to make her husband a quilt, and by chance, she had seen the copy of *Peterson's Magazine*. The coincidence seemed fortuitous. At first, she had thought she would line the quilt with wool. She would procure it from a neighbor who raised sheep, trading with him for a bushel or two of corn. The wool would be warmer than cotton. But then she thought down would be even warmer and not weigh so much. She'd never heard of anyone using down for batting, but it would be soft, and lightweight, too. So she killed and plucked the ducks and made a case of muslin the size of the quilt top, quilted it to keep the down in place. Then she layered the down pouch between quilt top and backing and quilted again, in the shapes of stars and oak leaves.

Eliza hefted the quilt and was pleased at its light weight. She turned the coverlet over and around, and ran her hand across the bottom until she could feel the name that was stitched just above the binding: "William Thomas Spooner, Wabaunsee County, Kansas, 1864." She had embroidered her husband's name so that no one else could claim the cover. And because stitching

Will's name pleased her. She had added her own name, too: Eliza Spooner.

A coyote howled, and there was a rustling in the chicken coop. Eliza set down the quilt and went to where the birds were roosting, but the pen was closed tight against the coyotes and the foxes and other predators that fancied poultry for supper, although not against tramps. She had seen her share of homeless men wandering the roads. Now that the cold weather was coming on, she wondered if they would ask to sleep in the barn, or worse, not ask at all. Davy had rousted one man after a rainy night, and prodding with a pitchfork, had ordered him out. It had been too dark for the tramp to see that Davy was only a boy. So he had run off, leaving chicken feathers in the hay where he had slept, and out back of the barn, they found where he had butchered and roasted the chicken. There would be other wanderers, army deserters, discharged soldiers with arms in slings or arms gone altogether. Eliza didn't mind the men who came to the house at dinnertime, begging a meal. They seemed harmless in the daytime, but she feared them after dark. She wished there were another man on the farm, but where could one find a hired man? And with what would she pay him if she did?

She made her way back to the house in the dark, pausing a little as she picked up the quilt and folded it, then held it against her chest. If Will were there, he would come outside to see what was keeping her, might put an arm around her, and they would stand silently, looking up at the stars and counting their blessings. It was a good life, and it would be again. Will would come home older, gray in his beard, perhaps a little more solemn. But he would brag he had saved the Union and would take down the fiddle, and they would sing the Yankee songs. And Eliza would silently thank God that her husband had come through safely. He would come home. Eliza had no doubt of it. He had promised.

With a frown at her useless daydreaming, Eliza went into the house and slid the board into place across the door, securing the cabin. She set the quilt on the table. First thing in the morning, she would take it to Enoch Coldridge, who had come home on furlough and would leave that week to return to the Kansas Volunteers. Enoch had agreed to take the quilt to Will, along with a sack of divinity candy, on which she'd used the last of her sugar, and the black walnuts she and the children had gathered only the week before. Eliza had her doubts that Will would ever see the divinity, but she depended on Enoch at least to deliver the quilt.

It was a stroke of luck that Enoch had come to call, had come just at suppertime to deliver a letter from Will. The supper had been meager, and Eliza had given up her portion to Enoch. He knew it and was beholden to her, so when she asked him to take the quilt back with him, he couldn't turn her down. If it weren't for Enoch, Eliza would have had to mail it, and who knew when it would arrive? Or if? With Enoch carrying it with him, the quilt would reach Will before Christmas. She had never given Will a Christmas present, and the idea of a special gift to her husband-soldier delighted Eliza. A quilt made with loving hands, a quilt that would warm Will against the winter cold, a quilt for Christmas.

CHAPTER ONE

Christmas Eve, 1864

The postmaster handed Eliza the letter the day before Christmas. It had sat in the box for a week, waiting for her, he said. "I'd have sent it along, but nobody was going out your way. I figured you'd be in for the oranges. I set two aside for you, the best two." The man operated the post office out of his general store.

The oranges were the reason Eliza had hitched old Sabra to the wagon and driven into town. She had a sack of corn in the back to trade, a steep price for two oranges, but it couldn't be helped. There were no coins to be spent. Will had promised to send her his thirteen dollars a month pay, but so far, she'd received nothing.

"It's from Will, is it not?" the postmaster asked, fingering the letter as if it were his own.

"It is." Eliza snatched the missive, as if she feared the man would open and read it himself. Perhaps he had already, for the letter was not sealed with wax but merely folded into itself, forming its own envelope.

But the postmaster didn't comment on the contents. "A nice Christmas present for you, then. I'll fetch them oranges."

Eliza nodded. The oranges were likely not the best ones at all but the culls, dull orange in color, shriveled, the juice half gone. But they were oranges, and it wouldn't be Christmas without them. She had told the children there might not be oranges this year, what with the war. After all, oranges came from somewhere in the South, so maybe the storekeeper wouldn't be able to get them. Davy and Luzena had said they understood, but she knew they would be disappointed. They had always had oranges at Christmas. When they were younger, Davy and Luzena would consume the fruit all at once, letting the juice run down their fingers, but now that they were older, they carefully savored each section so that the orange lasted the entire Christmas day. And they saved the peels for their mother to dry, then chop up for her cooking. Once Davy had cut his orange in half and scraped out the pulp with his teeth. Then he had fastened each half of the cleaned orange to the bottom of a bottle, where it dried hard into a cup. He'd hidden the cups a whole year, until the following Christmas, giving one to Luzena, the other to Eliza, who used it for her pins.

This year they would have the Christmas oranges after all, along with the divinity candy that Eliza had set aside when she made the batch for Will, had secreted it in a tin for a surprise. She would stew the rooster she had killed that morning and add potatoes and onions, mix in a few herbs she had collected and dried in the summer. And then she would surprise the children with the presents—a knife for Davy that Will had found on the road just before he left. Eliza had rubbed the rust from the knife, then polished it until it looked almost new. And there was a wooden doll for Luzena, although she was nearly too old for such a plaything. Will had carved the doll before he left for a soldier, and had given it to Eliza to hide. She'd made an indigo dress for the doll and wrapped it in a tiny quilt made from scraps left over from the Stars and Stripes quilt. Now, best of all, there would be Will's letter to read. She wouldn't open the letter until Christmas morning. They would read it before church.

As she left the store, the letter and the oranges safe in her basket, Eliza scanned the sky, thinking the three of them might not make it to church at all. The snow had threatened even before she set out for town, and she had worried that it might come quickly and make the driving difficult. But a snowstorm would not have kept her from the Christmas oranges.

The snow was coming fast, in flakes as big and as soft as the down in Will's Christmas quilt. As she hurried to the wagon, Eliza wondered if he had received it. She smiled to think that Will would spend the night before Christmas wrapped in the down-filled quilt she had made for him. She wondered if he would rub his hand against his name and hers and know how much she had loved stitching them, how much she loved him. She climbed into the wagon and flicked the reins against Sabra's back, and the horse started up, taking a quick step or two before settling into a walk. The horse was old, and Eliza was grateful the mare could pull the wagon at all.

As she slapped the reins against Sabra's back a second time, she heard someone shout, "Eliza!" and reined in the horse. She turned to the voice, unsure in the snow who was speaking to her.

"It's me, Missouri Ann Stark," a young woman said, emerging from the store and coming up to the wagon. "I saw you in the post office. I guess you didn't see me." Missouri Ann was small and pretty, with green eyes and hair so pale it was almost the white of the snow. But her face was gray and gaunt.

"I ask you to forgive me. There was a letter from Will, and for just about a minute, I forgot where I was." Eliza saw that her friend was clutching her own envelope. "Did you hear from Hugh, too? That would make Christmas all the better if we both got letters."

Missouri Ann shook her head. "Hugh can't write. Couldn't."

Eliza stared at the woman. "What do you mean, *couldn't?*"

"Oh, Eliza, Hugh's dead. I'm a widow woman." She stopped, as if studying the words, and repeated them. "I'm a widow woman. I don't have a husband no more." She rubbed her shawl across her face, then steadied herself. "It says right here in this letter that Hugh's killed hisself in the battle. They's wrote he died. Here, I'll read it to you. 'Missus Stark, your husband was perfectly resigned to dying. His final words were, "I die for a worthy cause." He died a-praising the Union and said for you not to worry because he was going to a better place.' "

"Do you believe it?" Eliza blurted out. She shouldn't have asked such a thing, but those were not words Hugh Stark would have spoken. More likely in his final moments, he would have profaned the Lord as well as the Union Army for playing such a rotten trick on him as to let him pass over.

"No, but it's nice they wrote it." She looked up, her face damp, but whether the wetness came from tears or snow Eliza didn't know. "Oh, Eliza, what's to become of us?"

"I'm sorry, Missouri Ann. It isn't fair the war's taken our men. I suppose you and Nance will stay on with the Starks." Eliza didn't like the Starks. They were loud and foulmouthed and lived like hogs. Hugh's brothers were too unpatriotic or too

24

cowardly to join the army. After they married, Hugh and Missouri Ann had gone to house-keeping on their own place, but when Hugh joined up, he moved his wife and daughter in with his family. Eliza had called on her friend only once at the Stark farm, because she could sense Missouri Ann's embarrassment at the way her husband's family lived. They were lazy and stupid, without sense enough to put butter on bread. Eliza couldn't think how they kept themselves, because nothing ever hatched on their farm.

"I can't. I'm between a hawk and a buzzard. They won't let me go, but I can't stay. They treat me like chicken scratch, and with Hugh dead, his brothers likely . . . Only thing protected me was they knew Hugh'd womp them if they didn't treat me right."

"But they're family. And surely they dote on Nance." Missouri Ann's daughter was not quite two. She was a pretty thing, with fine golden hair and hazel eyes.

"Not so's you'd notice. Only Mother Stark does. The men blame me she's not a boy."

"So you'll go back to your own people, then?"

"I can't. When I married Hugh, my folks said I couldn't never come home again."

"But they didn't mean it."

"They did, all right. They wouldn't take me in if it was snowing ice cakes and I was dressed naked."

25

Eliza understood. Missouri Ann's family was as judgmental as the Starks were mean.

"Oh, Eliza, I thought about it, 'course, thought what I'd do if Hugh got killed in the war, but never did I come up with a plan."

Eliza got out of the wagon and put her arms around Missouri Ann. "Do you have to tell the Starks that Hugh's dead? You could wait until you've found a place for you and Nance."

"I wish I'd thought of that. But I told the postmaster what was in the letter, and you know how you can't never trust him to keep a secret. Besides, Dad Stark gets the paper from Topeka every week where it lists the dead. He has me read it to him, for he can't read, neither. And how am I going to just skip over Hugh's name if it's there?"

Missouri Ann tucked the letter into the bosom of her dress and wiped her face with her hands. "I guess I should be mourning Hugh instead of worrying about me and Nance, but I can't help it. I got to think of us first. Mourning's for rich folks."

"Have you prayed?" Eliza said, and immediately regretted the words. When would Missouri Ann have prayed? She'd just received the letter. Besides, Missouri Ann hadn't been in church for a long time. She wasn't a praying woman.

"Me and the Lord ain't too acquainted of late."

"Maybe not, but surely someone at the church would find a place for you."

"Maybe you forgot Nance came awful early, and there's some that holds it against me, believes me to be a prodigal woman."

Eliza did remember now, but the gossiping had been more about Missouri Ann fornicating with a Stark than about the early arrival of the baby. The baby had been the only explanation Eliza could think of for why Missouri Ann, that sweet girl, had married Hugh. She hadn't wanted to have a briar-patch child, a bastard.

Missouri Ann looked Eliza square in the face and said, "I could come live with you."

"Me?"

The new widow had been holding her breath, and now she said in a rush, "You got that hired man's soddy out back of your house. I could work around the place to pay for lodging. And Nance won't be no trouble. We wouldn't be a burden to you."

"But it's a ramshackle house with a hole in the wall where the snow drifts in. That's no fit place for a woman and child."

"I'm a good fixer. You should have seen me at the Stark place, nailing up boards. I wanted it warm for Nance. I asked the boys, but they're lazy as summer rain. They don't do nothing and don't start that till after dinner. The roof on that cabin is awful bad, and Mother Stark complained the rain was coming in on her bed and asked them to do something about it. So they went upstairs and moved the bed. That's all the good they are, and her their mother, birthing and raising them. She was the only decent one in the lot."

Eliza laughed despite herself. She wondered again why Missouri Ann had married into such a family, why she'd fallen in love with Hugh Stark. Maybe it had been his good looks and the slow way he smiled. He'd seemed truly taken with Missouri Ann, however, and might have been a better man than she'd given him credit for, although she wasn't sure. And then she remembered that Hugh Stark's widow was standing in front of her. "He was a good husband. I'm sorry about Hugh, Missouri Ann. Truly I am."

Missouri Ann looked away. "Like I say, I can't think about that now. I got to ponder what I'm going to do. I best have plans before the Starks find out about Hugh. They might expect me to marry Edison."

The woman had said that last in such a low voice that Eliza had strained to hear her, and even then, she wasn't sure she had heard right. "Marry Edison? Edison Stark? Hugh's brother?"

"The same."

"One-legged Edison?"

Missouri Ann nodded.

"But why would you do that?"

"It might be I won't have a choice. You don't know the Starks, Eliza. Mother Stark said if anything happened to Hugh, I'd best get away fast, or it might be I'd never get another chance. She said it was too late for her, too late by thirty years, but I still had time. The Starks don't want me, but they won't let me go, neither."

Had Hugh been like the rest of them? Eliza wondered. Had the sins of his father passed on to him? But Missouri Ann cared for him, so maybe he was different.

"Hugh was the best of them," Missouri Ann said, as if she knew what Eliza was thinking. "He was a good man. I'll raise Nance to think well of her father." Then she added, "Maybe I could stay with old Aunt Grace. She needs someone to have a care for her."

Old Aunt Grace was a slattern who lived in a shack in the woods and trapped wild animals, eating their flesh and selling their skins.

"No," Eliza said, horrified. "You'll move in with us." She said it quickly, without much thought, but now she realized she had no choice but to take in Missouri Ann and Nance. What if Will had been killed and she and the children had had to leave the farm? Where would they have gone? "We would welcome you and Nance, Missouri Ann."

Missouri Ann stared at Eliza. "You sure?"

Eliza said they would go and get Missouri

Ann's things right then, before the storm got worse.

"Cain't. I'll have to sneak away. I'll walk to your place."

"In this snow?" Eliza thought a moment, then said they could meet at church the following day.

Missouri Ann frowned. "Starks don't go to church, even at Christmas."

"Then you must tell them you are going to church for Nance's sake," Eliza said. "What about your belongings?"

"Ain't got any," Missouri Ann said.

As she rode behind the slow horse back to the farm, Eliza wondered what had happened to her friend in the past few years. She'd been shocked, of course, when Missouri Ann married Hugh Stark. He was a comely man with a smile that would have melted ice in midwinter, but there had been something about him that Eliza feared. Missouri Ann had been raised by a family of holy willies whose only joy was pointing out the sins of others. Eliza's friend knew from an early age she was going to hell, so what did it matter if she broke a few of God's laws, especially the one about fornication? But with a Stark! Missouri Ann was guileless and good. She could have done better. And then to be dumped at the Stark shanty when Hugh went off to war! Missouri Ann was a tough girl, but she had grown depressed, beaten down in the last months. Well, who wouldn't be, living with a family like that? Eliza chided herself for not having been a better friend. Then she wondered if Missouri Ann had any friends at all or whether, like Eliza, they'd been dis-couraged from visiting.

Of course Eliza would let Missouri Ann and Nance live at the Spooner farm. She wondered that she had hesitated at all. Things would be tight. They would all have to be careful to make the food last through the winter. The harvest had been all right, although even with the help of men working on shares, they had had to leave some of the crops to rot. Eliza had tried to persuade Will to wait to join up until after the harvest was over, but he was anxious to kill the Rebels. He'd said she could manage, and she had, although not as well as if he'd been there.

Even if Hugh's pay came through, there would be little money for necessities and none for extravagances such as more oranges. It was doubtful Missouri Ann would bring so much as a penny with her. But they would make it. Having another woman living on the place might help the loneliness she had felt since Will enlisted. And Eliza and the children would be safer with another adult there. She'd worried about safety ever since Davy found that tramp in the barn.

31

The cold had begun to seep into Eliza's bones, and she tried to hurry the horse, but Sabra couldn't be persuaded to pick up speed. Eliza hoped the Stark horse was faster, because she didn't like to think about baby Nance out in the cold. She had glimpsed the child peering out of the window where Missouri Ann had left her when she came out of the store to hail Eliza. Then Eliza realized there hadn't been another horse tied to the rail next to Sabra. Unless one of the Starks had driven her into town, which wasn't likely, Missouri Ann had walked to the store, tramping through the snow with her baby. Now she would be hurrying back in her thin shawl, carrying the little one. Not for the first time did Eliza thank God for giving her such a good life, such a good husband.

Eliza did not tell the children about Missouri Ann and Nance for fear they might mention to someone at church that the two were moving to the Spooner farm. She heard Davy and Luzena get up early, giggling, tiptoeing to her bed to see if she was sleeping. Eliza kept her eyes closed until Luzena crawled into bed beside her and asked in a loud whisper, "Aren't you awake, Mama?"

"Why, it's early yet. Go back to bed. What possesses the two of you to rise so far from dawn?"

"It's Christmas, Mama," Davy told her.

"Why, so it is. I forgot."

"You didn't forget," Luzena said. "There's two oranges on the table that weren't there last night."

"I wonder where they came from," Eliza said.

"From you!" Davy told her. "You said you couldn't get them, but we knew you would."

"There's something else for you, from your father," Eliza told them, pushing back the quilts and stepping into her shoes. "Why, son, you already built the fire."

Davy shrugged. "Papa always did it before you got up. I guess I can now. That's my Christmas present to you."

Eliza dressed quickly and went to the pie safe, taking out the makings for breakfast. While she mixed the porridge in a black iron pot, which she hung on a crane over the fire, Davy cut slices of bread and put them on a fork to toast over the coals.

"What else? What else did Papa get us for Christmas?" Luzena asked, as she placed forks on the table. She removed a candle from a tin box—the candles were stored there so the mice wouldn't gnaw them—then set the family Bible next to it.

"First, we thank the Lord," Eliza said. The three bowed their heads, while Eliza gave thanks for their food and asked that Will be safely returned to them. When she was finished, she picked up the Bible to read the Christmas story, but the children fidgeted so that she decided the reading could wait. She told Luzena, "Fetch me my sewing basket." The girl jumped up and returned with the basket. Eliza reached into its bottom, underneath a piece of fabric, and removed the doll. "Your papa made it," she told Luzena, who shrieked at the sight of the wooden toy.

"It looks just like me," she said, stroking the corn-silk hair that Eliza had attached to the doll's head. "She has a dress like mine and a quilt like Papa's." Luzena sat down and began examining the doll's clothes.

"And this is for you, Davy." Eliza handed the knife to her son.

"Swell!" he said, fingering the blade.

Luzena looked up from her doll, then. "There's nothing for you, Mama."

"Oh yes there is. I have a letter from your father right here. I picked it up yesterday and decided to wait until Christmas Day to read it." She stood and removed the letter from the mantel where she had placed it the night before, then slowly unfolded it, thinking that Will's hands had been the last to touch the precious page. She pictured him in the candlelight of his tent or maybe perched on a rock in the winter sun, pencil in hand, thinking of her as he set down the words. She glanced at the salutation and read the first line to herself.

"Read it out loud," Luzena demanded. She removed the doll's white apron and ironed it between her fingers.

Eliza smiled at Davy and Luzena, then began to read.

December 5, 1864
My Beloved Eliza & children

Eliza's voice caught, and she paused a moment to get control of herself. She had tried hard to keep the children from knowing how much she missed their father, how worried she was for his safety—and for their own future.

"What does he say?" Davy asked.

She began again.

My Beloved Eliza & children,
I take this opportunity to tell you I am well & hearty & that Enoch delivered your quilt this evening. I immediately put it to use, to the joy of my pards. It is as fine a quilt as ever was. The other soldiers envy my good fortune in having such a thoughtful wife. No one in camp has ever seen such a patriotic quilt. I am glad my name is on it, else it would be stole. There never was a wife as good as you.

Eliza paused to savor the compliments. She knew they would be followed with instructions, maybe criticisms, and they were.

Keep a good account of money matters, & do not be tempted to spend foolishly.

As if she would, Eliza thought.

It is said we will do battle with the Secesh tomorrow, & I expect we will whip them, for they are cowardly fools who do not deserve the name of men. I never detested a group of human beings so much. There is no man so wicked as one who holds another in bondage & I believe there is not a single Johnny Reb I could admire. I expect to dispatch a number of them to hell. I ask your prayers that we kill every last one of them.

I am glad you have finished the harvest. It should not have taxed you too much. Sell the excess, & keep the money in a safe place. I will be home in time for planting if we beat the G—d d——d Johnnies. Tell Davy I will get a Rebel for him.

The weather has turned cold. I thank you again for the quilt. I will think of you each night, dear wife, until we can sleep under it together. I pray the Lord will provide for you & our country.

Tell the children to have faith in God & love their mother. Keep in good spirits & all will be well.

Until I see you again, I hold you in my heart.
Your Affectionate Husband
William T. Spooner

Eliza held the letter over her own heart for a moment and shut her eyes to keep the tears from falling. It was the best letter she had ever received from Will. She suddenly thought of what Missouri Ann had told her, that her husband couldn't write, and so she would have no final letter from him, no letters at all, in fact.

"Will Papa really kill a Rebel for me?" Davy asked. "I hate them as much as he does, maybe more, because they will try to kill him."

"We don't hate anyone," Eliza replied, wishing Will had not been so outspoken in the letter.

"Well, I do. I hate the Secesh, and I hope Papa kills a peck of them!"

"It is Christmas Day, Davy, a day of love, not hate," Eliza said. "Now go milk Bossie, and I'll hitch Sabra to the wagon. We will go to church."

"In the snow?"

"We'll take the sleigh," Eliza said, suddenly remembering the vehicle, and the children clapped their hands. She had forgotten about the sleigh, which Will had acquired the previous winter from an undertaker who was passing through. The man had learned the new art of embalming, which was being used to treat the Union dead—

the wealthy ones, at any rate—and was going to Colorado to try his luck with the miners. "It's terrible accidents they have in the mines. I can make the dead look like they're only sleeping, fix them so's they can be shipped back home. A body embalmed by me never turns black," he had said. The man was from the South and thought the land west of the Missouri would be covered in snow, so he'd had a sleigh fitted up in Kansas City. But he had discovered the prairie was bare dirt, and so he'd traded the sleigh to Will for a rickety wagon.

The sleigh was a pretty thing, painted red with gold designs and EMBALMERS OF THE DEAD in black and gold letters on the side. Eliza had intended to paint out the words, but she hadn't gotten around to it. Some might think it sacrilegious to ride to church with that lettering on the sleigh on Christmas Day, but she believed God enjoyed a laugh, even if some of the parishioners didn't. Still, she would have to paint out the words before Easter. "Embalmers of the Dead" wouldn't be funny on the day Jesus rose from the dead. But then, Easter was in the spring, too late for a sleigh ride.

"Davy, you do the milking quick now, while I hitch up the horse. Luzena, put bricks in the hearth. We'll wrap them in blankets to keep our feet warm."

"How will we keep our feet warm after

church?" the girl asked, a reasonable question. "We can sing hymns and stamp our feet as we drive back."

"I'd rather sing 'When Papa Comes Marching Home,'" Davy said. Eliza had taught the song to the children, substituting "Papa" for "Johnny."

I would, too, Eliza thought, as she donned her cloak and headed for the barn.

The snow had stopped in the night, and the ground was covered with a foot of white. The sun glinted on it, making Eliza squint as she made her way to the barn. Perhaps she should put black under her eyes to keep the glare from hurting them. But she couldn't arrive at church on Christmas Day looking like a raccoon.

On occasion, she was just a little vain. And with good reason. At thirty-three, she was still a beauty. Her black hair had only a few strands of white—like stars on a dark night, Will had told her. Despite the birth of Davy and Luzena and two babies afterward who hadn't lived, she retained the figure she'd had on her wedding day fifteen years earlier. She was faithful about wearing her sunbonnet, so her face was still pale and unwrinkled, although her hands, she had to admit, were rough from hard work. She prided herself on her straight back, which made her look even taller than her five-foot-seven-inch height. She took a kind of perverse pride in being too tall to be fashionable. They were a couple who stood above the crowd, Will had observed, for he was near six feet himself.

Eliza had always known she would marry him. They had grown up together, had both attended the little school at the bottom of the hill of his grandparents' farm in Ohio. It was assumed by their families, too, that they would marry. What no one assumed was that the couple would leave Ohio for Kansas. But Will was restless among so much family. Although Eliza was content to stay with her people, Will had wanted to try for Oregon. Then a friend told him of the vast prairies west of the Missouri just waiting to be broken by a plow. So the two had headed for Kansas. If Kansas didn't suit, they could go to Oregon later on. But although Eliza had missed the lushness of Ohio and its pretty white buildings set on shady streets, Will had loved the rolling hills and golden prairie and announced they were home.

Life hadn't been easy, especially at first. They had lived in a house made of strips of sod, and there had been rattlesnakes—and Indians. At first, Eliza had been terrified of the red men. One day, when Will was in the fields, three Indian men had ridden up to the soddy. She had been outside with the children, baking in the outdoor oven that Will had constructed for her. The Indians rode between her and the house, and there was no way she could reach it, to barricade herself inside with the children.

So swallowing her fright, she removed a pan of cornbread from the oven and boldly took it to the men. "Cornbread," she cried, as if the Indians were deaf. "Help yourselves." She held up the pan, and the three Indians scooped out the cornbread with their hands, stuffing it into their mouths.

"Ko-fee," one of them said. He pointed to the soddy and dismounted.

Walking slowly with the children hanging on to her skirts, she went inside with the Indian and picked up the pot with the remains of the morning coffee. She usually made plenty in the morning so that she could reheat it for dinner. "Cold," she said, as she poured the coffee into a tin cup. "Cold coffee."

"Cold ko-fee," the Indian said. He drank it down, and Eliza refilled the cup. "Cold ko-fee good." He handed the cup to the second Indian. As they left, one of the men took a tiny scrap of fabric from his braided hair and dropped it on the ground at Eliza's feet. It was a beautiful shade of indigo, and Eliza had kept it for years, until she incorporated it into the Stars and Stripes Quilt.

"You did the right thing," Will told her later that day. "They're friendlies. No need to be afraid of them. Why, you see, he gave you a present. He must know you like to quilt."

The Indians returned from time to time, asking

for "cold ko-fee good." Once they were accompanied by an Indian woman, who looked at Eliza shyly, silently, then peered inside the soddy and stared in wonder. She glanced up at the ceiling, at the quilt frame Will had made and suspended from the ceiling on ropes so that Eliza could lower it in the evenings to sew. There had been no room in the house to set up a quilt frame, so Will had come up with the idea of hanging it high up.

Eliza lowered the frame, then removed the old piece of muslin that she used to cover her quilt so that dirt from the ceiling didn't fall onto it. The Indian woman ran her hand over the fabrics, pointing at the different colors, as Eliza named them in English.

The Indian woman was silent until Eliza pointed to a bright red fabric. "Red," she said.

"Red," the woman repeated, the first word she had spoken since she'd arrived.

On impulse, Eliza removed a swatch of the fabric from her sewing basket and handed it to the Indian. "For you," she said.

"For you," the woman repeated solemnly.

They had lived in the soddy until Will built the two-story log house with a board floor, and now the old place was the hired man's cabin—or had been in the years they had had enough money to hire a man. That was where Missouri Ann and Nance would live. It would take a little fixing, but when that was done, the soddy would be tight and cozy. Of course, Missouri Ann and Nance were welcome to live in the big house with Eliza and the children, but Eliza had a feeling that her friend would rather be by herself. Missouri Ann had lived with the Starks long enough to value her privacy.

Eliza smiled as she rode out of the barn in the sleigh. Luzena ran from the house with the hot bricks wrapped in an old quilt and placed them on the floor of the sleigh. Then Davy emerged from the milk house and climbed in so that Eliza had a child on either side of her.

As she flicked the reins on Sabra's back and the old horse started off, Eliza told the children that she had another surprise.

"What?" the two asked together.

"It's a secret until after church," she replied, then wondered if she should have kept silent. Maybe Missouri Ann wouldn't show up.

CHAPTER TWO

Christmas Day, 1864

Despite the cold and the snow, the yard of the little church was crowded with wagons, sleighs, and buggies, horses stamping their feet, their breath coming out in streams of white in the cold air. Except for the evergreens and sleigh bells on the door, the little white church was almost invisible against the white snow.

Davy and Luzena ran off to find their friends and tell them about their Christmas gifts, while Eliza looked around for Missouri Ann. Her friend was not with the group of parishioners gathered by the vehicles, who were greeting one another with cries of "Happy Christmas." Nor was Missouri Ann inside. Perhaps the Starks had decided to come to church after all and were late. But Eliza could not recall the Starks ever attending church and thought it was more likely that they had discovered Missouri Ann's plans to leave and were keeping her at home. Eliza pondered what she would do if that were so. It wasn't as though she could drive up to the Stark place in the undertaker's sleigh and rescue her friend. Perhaps Missouri Ann herself had decided to stay on with her in-laws. Maybe she had concluded life with the Starks was preferable to living in a rundown soddy on an isolated farm. But Eliza didn't think so.

Eliza called to the children, and the three of them went inside, sitting in the family pew toward the front of the church. Eliza still felt odd attending the service without Will—incomplete. He always sat at the end of the pew, as if protecting his family. Now Eliza was in that place. Perhaps she should yield the spot to Davy. No, Eliza thought, Davy was too young to take on the responsibility of a man. He was a boy, Will had insisted when Davy begged to join the army as a drummer boy.

When she glanced around at the congregation, Eliza realized she was not the only war widow in the church. The conflict had taken away so many of the men, some dead, some still fighting, a few whose status was unknown. That last was what she feared most, that Will would simply disappear and she would never know what had happened to him. At least Missouri Ann had been notified that Hugh was dead. She could grieve properly. Eliza glanced around the church, thinking Missouri Ann might have sneaked in during the service, but there was no sign of her.

The parishioners were singing the "Old One

Hundred" when Eliza felt a rush of cold air. She turned to see that the door had opened and that Missouri Ann and Nance had slipped inside. Nance, eyes downcast in shyness, tottered beside her mother as Missouri Ann walked quietly down the aisle. Eliza and the children crowded together to make room for the two in the Spooner pew. Missouri Ann's long skirts were soaked, and Eliza knew she had tramped through the snow for miles to reach the church. She grasped Missouri Ann's raw hand and thought it felt like ice. Others saw Missouri Ann enter the church, and as the word had got out that Hugh Stark was dead, several tried to catch the woman's eye and give her nods of sympathy. Even those who remembered Nance had come early would give no looks of disdain to the new widow on that holy day.

The service was a short one, perhaps because it was Christmas and the congregation was anxious to return home to what might be their only feast for many months. While the harvest had been good, people had encountered shortages during the war, so they were frugal. These were squally times. Or maybe the minister was afraid that the snow would start again and trap the congregation on the roads.

At the end of the closing prayer, the door banged open again, and a voice said, "There she is, pious as a priest. I told you to stay to home, girl. Why'd you run off for? You come here, you know what's good for you."

Eliza knew without turning that the voice came from one of the Starks and that it was directed at Missouri Ann. Holding tight to Nance, Missouri Ann cringed against Eliza, as Dad Stark came up and grabbed the woman's arm, three of his sons trailing behind him. There had been a dozen or so Stark boys—poor Mother Stark had had them like rabbits—but half had either lit out or hadn't lived to grow up.

"I'm not going," Missouri Ann said, shivering against Eliza.

Dad Stark glared at his daughter-in-law. He was a big man. He might have been handsome once, but he smelled bad, and his hair and beard had grown thick and long and snarled, so that he looked like a cat's dinner. "What's that you say?" he growled. "I'll have no back talk from you."

"We've got shut of you. Me and Nance ain't going to live with you no more."

"You got to. Who'll read the names in the newspaper? What if one of my boys died? How'd I know?"

"You ain't got any more boys in the war," Missouri Ann told him. "Hugh's the only one joined up."

"You watch your mouth," Dad Stark told her. "You belong to us."

"I don't belong to nobody. You treat me mean,

47

make me clean up your messes and not give me no more to eat than a slave."

"Mr. Lincoln freed the slaves," Eliza spoke up.

"I guess she ain't a slave then. She's just a woman. And women got no rights." Dad Stark glanced at Eliza, who gave him a furious look, and he took a step back and asked, "Who're you?"

Eliza didn't answer his question. Instead she said, "Missouri Ann doesn't have to live with you if she doesn't want to. You don't own her."

"By rights I do. She's my son's wife, ain't she, and since he's dead, she passes on to me. She's going to marry Edison."

"I won't!" Missouri Ann said.

"We already decided. If you don't marry him, who's going to take care of him? Tell me that. Besides, ain't nobody else wants you. Who'd take you in?"

"I would," Eliza said. As Dad Stark stared at her dumbfounded, Eliza stood and faced him. "Missouri Ann and Nance are moving in with me." Eliza looked at him defiantly, although inside, she was knotted up. She'd never confronted a man like that, especially in front of so many people. Will didn't think much of women who spoke out in public, but Will wasn't there to speak for her.

"Who's us?"

"I'm Mrs. William Spooner."

48

"Her husband's gone off to the war, too," Taft, one of the sons, said. "You know what them grass widows do with their time."

Eliza turned red at the suggestion she was entertaining men and wanted to sink down in the pew and cover her face with her hands, but denying the words would have no more effect than ignoring them. Besides, she was more concerned about Missouri Ann than herself. She did not want to be sidetracked by the false charges when Missouri Ann needed her to remain calm.

Dad Stark clenched his fists. "That the kind of woman you are, Missouri Ann? Hugh'd rather see you cold in the ground than a wanton woman."

"I ain't nothing like that, me or Eliza Spooner, neither. You got no call to accuse me, Dad Stark. I'm a good woman."

The old man grabbed Missouri Ann's arm and yanked her up. She tried to pull away, but her father-in-law held her firmly and began dragging her down the aisle.

"Just a minute there, Mr. Stark."

Eliza had been so intent on watching Dad Stark and his sons that she hadn't seen the minister come down the aisle. John Hamlin wasn't a full-time preacher, only a volunteer. He was the most learned man in Wabaunsee County and some thought the most righteous, a man who it was rumored had operated a stop on the Underground

Railroad during slavery days. He was also a banker and the richest man in the county, and people deferred to him for those reasons if for no other. Since the congregation couldn't afford a regular minister, John Hamlin had been asked to fill in on Sundays. Now Reverend Hamlin, as he was called, put his hand on Dad Stark's arm and said evenly, "I believe we can indeed see what kind of women these are, and so can the Lord. They are pleasing in His sight."

The reverend paused to make sure he had Dad Stark's attention. "You have no call to accuse these good women of compromising themselves. You have embarrassed all the ladies of this congregation with your slander. Your daughter-in-law is a new widow and filled with grief, and instead of offering the deepest sympathy and consolation, you are adding to her misery. I believe you are grieving, too, and that is the only reason we will excuse your talk. But it must stop. This is Christmas Day, and we are here to celebrate the birth of our Lord, Jesus Christ. You and your sons are welcome to join with us if you will sit down in a pew and take a prayerful attitude. Otherwise, we must ask you to leave."

"How's that?" Dad Stark asked. It was unlikely anyone had chastised him before—or ever invited him to a church service.

"And afterward you will say good-bye to Mrs. Missouri Ann, and wish her well, and she will be allowed to go wherever she chooses," the minister continued.

"Why, you can't tell me what to do, a puny little feller like you. I'd squash you with the back of my hand," Dad Stark said. He rolled around a chaw of tobacco in his mouth, then spat it onto the church floor. Eliza put her hand to her mouth in shock and disgust.

Reverend Hamlin didn't flinch, although he did look over the Stark brood, who outnumbered him four to one. "Do not threaten me in the Lord's House," he said softly.

Dad Stark grinned, but the grin faded as Print Ritter, a blacksmith built like an oak stump, rose and stood beside John Hamlin. "I stand with the reverend. You going to squash me, too, Stark?"

"Ain't got nothing to do with you, Ritter, or you, neither, Mr. Hamlin. This is twixt me and Hugh's wife."

"You're profaning the church where Mrs. Missouri Ann is a member, and like the preacher said, she's a grieving widow. I guess it has to do with me. It has to do with all of us." The blacksmith made a sweeping gesture with his hand that included the entire congregation—most of it anyway. While the majority of the worshipers nodded, here and there a few who did not approve of Missouri Ann looked down at their Bibles. Several men stood up and moved toward the aisle.

Stark glared at the parishioners, then turned to his sons. "I guess we're outnumbered. We could take 'em in a fair fight, but this one ain't fair." He shook Missouri Ann's arm, then dropped it. "This ain't over with, you hear, Missouri Ann?"

"Yes, it is over," the reverend said. "Mrs. Missouri Ann is free to do what she likes, and if any harm comes to her or those who help her, you will answer to this entire congregation."

Dad Stark scoffed, probably thinking that while the churchgoers might be lined up against him that day when they were all together, it was unlikely they cared enough about Missouri Ann to form a vigilante party later on to go after the Starks. "We'll see about that," he said.

"And you will answer to me personally."

At that, one of the Stark boys let out a loud laugh. "Why, I could pound you in the ground with my big toe."

"Perhaps you could. But do I have to remind you gentlemen that I hold a mortgage on your farm, and I believe you have a payment due on January first?" He paused, then added, "January first of 1864. God bless me, that means you are nearly a year late. And another payment is due on January first next year, just one week from now. I hate to take away anyone's farm, but . . ." He shrugged.

The Starks looked at each other, but before they could respond, the reverend turned and walked back to the pulpit, saying, "Now, friends, our closing hymn is 'All Hail the Power.' "

The Starks glared at Missouri Ann, who ignored them and began singing in her sweet voice. She glanced sidelong at Eliza, as the entire Stark family clumped down the aisle, swearing and pounding the floor with their heavy feet.

By the time the service was over, the Starks had cleared out. There was no sign of them in the church yard.

"Thank you, Reverend," Missouri Ann told the minister as she curtsied to him at the doorway. "If you hadn't spoken up, they'd have hauled me back to that awful place, and me and Nance would never have got away."

"Oh, don't thank me. I wouldn't have done you much good in a fight. But Print there, I believe he could have taken on the whole family and beaten them with one hand." The reverend cleared his throat. "Such talk on this holy day. You must forgive me. Happy Christmas to you, ladies."

Eliza led the way to the sleigh, Missouri Ann and the children behind her. The cutter was designed for two, so it would be a tight fit. Just as they reached the sleigh, Print Ritter came up. Missouri Ann seemed tongue-tied, so Eliza said, "We are grateful to you, Mr. Ritter. If you hadn't stood up beside Reverend Hamlin, I believe the Starks might have dragged Missouri Ann out of church."

The blacksmith looked uncomfortable. "I don't like seeing a person mistreated, especially by the likes of the Starks. I'm glad you're shut of them, ma'am." He lifted his hat to Missouri Ann, who blushed and mumbled her thanks. "And I'm real sorry that Hugh got killed." He didn't look sorry. Missouri Ann thanked him again in a low voice, and he added, "If them fellows bother you again, you just let me know. I'll take care of them."

"We will," Eliza said.

The blacksmith glanced at Missouri Ann, but she was too embarrassed to look up.

"You think the Starks'll join up with the Union and maybe go away?" Davy asked, when the five were crowded into the sleigh and Eliza had spread a quilt over them. The bricks for their feet had long since gone cold.

Missouri Ann shook her head. "They're copperheads!" she whispered, as if the words could not be spoken aloud.

"You mean they don't support the Union?" Davy asked, astonishment in his voice.

"That's what I'm saying."

"But Hugh joined up with the Kansas Volunteers," Eliza told her.

"Oh, Hugh was different," Missouri Ann said. "Your daddy was a fine man," she told Nance, who was cuddled in her arms.

"Maybe his brothers will join the Confederate army then," Eliza said.

"They're too cowardly."

Davy laughed at that. "Papa says all the Confederates are cowards. That's why we'll beat them." Then he added, "The Starks backed down awful fast when Mr. Ritter stood up to them."

Missouri Ann seemed to think that over and looked out at the snow-covered land with a slight smile on her face. The snow hadn't started again, but the wind had come up, and the faces of the five were red and cold. "They got what they deserved."

"Do you think they'll trouble us?" Eliza asked. "Maybe they'll come looking for you at the farm."

"Not considerable trouble," Missouri Ann replied. "They wouldn't do that."

"I guess Mr. Ritter scared them away," Eliza suggested.

"It ain't that. They ain't got the money to pay the mortgage, and they're scared they'll lose the place, poor as it is."

"So we have nothing to worry about," Eliza said.

"Oh, I didn't say that. The Starks is too mean to give up. They'll bother us some, maybe steal chickens or break down a fence. We have to keep a watch for them. But they wouldn't burn down the house or steal me and Nance."

"And if they did, I'd go after them with Papa's gun," Davy said.

Eliza turned to stare at her son, suddenly realizing he wasn't a child anymore. Davy was almost as tall as Eliza, and his voice had changed. Some boys no older than he had joined the army as drummers, a few even as soldiers. With four females living on the farm now, Davy really was the man of the house. Eliza decided that on the next Sunday, her son would take Will's place at the end of the pew.

Eliza had left a banked fire in the house, and when they returned from church, she and Davy added wood to the coals, and before long, the house was warm. She cut up the rooster she'd killed the day before and placed it with winter vegetables in an iron pot, which she hung from a crane over the fire. The children sat at the table, peeling their oranges and sharing them with Nance.

"One for me and one for you," Davy said, handing the child a section.

"One for me and one for you," Luzena repeated.

"That's not right," Davy said. "She's getting twice as many as we are."

Luzena frowned, not understanding. "Then I won't give her any more."

"No, that doesn't work out right, either."

"More," Nance said.

"She's never ate a orange before," Missouri Ann told Eliza.

"What about you?" Eliza asked.

Missouri Ann shook her head. "I seen them but never had the cash to buy one."

"Davy . . ." Eliza said, but her son had already gotten up from the table, and he gave Missouri Ann an orange section.

"Me, too," said Luzena, proffering her own bit of orange, but Missouri Ann shook her head, saying one piece was enough.

Missouri Ann ate her bit of orange slowly. "Tastes like summer," she said.

"It does at that," said Eliza, who was mixing dough for dumplings.

"You let me do that. You take a resting spell," Missouri Ann said.

Eliza shook her head. "We'll let that old rooster stew. It's time you saw the soddy. You'll have to sleep here with us until we get it fixed up. In fact, maybe you ought to stay here altogether."

"No, me and Nance can live in the soddy."

"Then let's get to it. Maybe you'll change your mind after you see it," Eliza told her, removing her shawl from a peg and opening the door. She led the way to a building built of long strips of prairie sod stacked on top of each other. The soddy was small and low to the ground, and there was a hole in the back wall. Eliza thought animals might have sheltered inside. She and Will had loved the little house, but they had been young and newly in love, and the soddy was their first home. It had been a cozy house, cool in summer and so warm in winter that she hadn't had to sleep with her bowl of yeast to keep it from freezing. Now she saw what a dismal place it really was. Clods of earth had fallen from the ceiling onto the floor. "It's awful dirty," Eliza said.

Missouri Ann laughed. "Of course it is. It's made of dirt, ain't it?" She clapped her hands. "Why, it's as fine a house as I ever lived in! And to think there's just the two of us. We'll get lost in here."

Eliza blinked at that, because the soddy was not much bigger than a horse stall. "It's awfully small."

"Just the right size. I can sit on the bed and flip pancakes."

"You can't stay here yet."

"I'll clean it up tomorrow. It don't need much work at all, just that hole in the side patched. Someday maybe I'll get me muslin to stretch across the ceiling so's the dirt don't fall down. It's a right fine house, best I ever saw." She frowned. "I didn't bring anything with me, not even a cookpot."

"I got extra," Eliza told her. "Extra dishes, too." She frowned and added, "But you won't need them. We'll all eat together."

"'Bliged. I wish I could have brought my scrap bag with me, but the Starks would have knowed for sure I was leaving if I'd taken that along to church. They know it means more to me than anything. Mean as they are, they probably've used it for kindling by now."

"The idea!" Eliza gasped. Then she asked, "You quilt then?"

"Of course I do. I'd rather quilt than eat cake on Sunday," Missouri Ann replied.

"Then we will make quite a pair. I've got enough scraps for both of us. We'll spend the winter piecing. It'll be like when I was young and sat with my mother and sisters over the quilt frame after the supper dishes were done and the bread set. There's nothing I'd rather do than quilt with another woman. I've got quilts in the house you can use until we've made some for you, although what I have is a poor offering."

"Oh, I wouldn't think so," Missouri Ann said. "You have the reputation of being the best quilter for miles around. Ain't nobody can quilt like you—except maybe me on my best day." She gave a sly grin that was almost a challenge.

"Then together, we'll make the best quilts anybody in Wabaunsee County's ever seen."

"That's a fact."

"I made a quilt for Will—my husband—for Christmas, you know," Eliza said, then wondered, how would Missouri Ann know?

"I do know. I met Enoch on the road as he was going back to the Kansas Volunteers. He told me."

"Was he eating divinity candy?" Eliza had to ask.

"He was at that."

"Well, at least Will got the quilt, and in time for Christmas. My husband wrote me. That was the letter I received yesterday."

"A letter from your husband. Ain't that romantic? I never got a letter in my life, except the one saying Hugh was dead."

Eliza found that strangely moving. She took her friend's hand and said, "I'm so sorry about Hugh, Missouri Ann."

"He was all right. I told Nance that. She'll be raised with the knowing that he was all right."

"He was, indeed," Eliza agreed, thinking there was nothing wrong with telling a little lie.

"He wasn't like the rest of the Starks. He wouldn't have treated me the way they did," Missouri Ann insisted.

"Of course not," Eliza replied. "I don't suppose he left you anything."

Missouri Ann shook her head. "Anything he had, Dad Stark's taken the possession of it."

Eliza nodded. "Then next week, we'll go to the postmaster and find out how you apply for a pension."

"A what?"

"A pension. When a man dies in the war, the army pays his widow a sum of money every month in compensation. Of course, money doesn't compensate for the loss of a husband. And it isn't much, maybe three dollars a month."

Missouri Ann thought that over. "I guess maybe that's another reason the Starks wanted me and Nance to stay. Three dollars a month is a fortune to them. To me, too."

"But it's not as much as Hugh was paid for being a soldier."

"Hugh got paid?" Missouri Ann's mouth dropped open. "I never saw a penny of it." Then she added quickly, "The Starks must have got it. Hugh wouldn't have left his wife and daughter without no money."

The children had gone to sleep as soon as supper was over, Luzena sharing her bed with Nance and the new doll, which she had named Miss Cat, for her pet who had died the year before. Missouri Ann had offered to sleep on the floor "like I done at the Starks'," she'd said, but Eliza insisted her friend share her own bed. "We'll keep each other warm," she'd told Missouri Ann, realizing how cold her bed had been with Will away. When she had dressed that morning at the Starks', Missouri Ann had slipped her dress over her nightgown, and now she was sleeping warm in that garment, covered by quilts.

Eliza was tired, too, but she was restless. She wondered what Will would think about her taking in Missouri Ann and Nance. Would he approve?

Of course he would. Will was a kind man. He'd taken in stray dogs and cats, and more than once, he'd asked her to give a meal to a tramp passing through. He wouldn't deny shelter to a woman and child. Still, she ought to ask for his permission. But what if he said no? Eliza smiled to herself. She'd ask in such a way that he couldn't turn her down. She'd done that often enough.

And so, despite the hour and her own weariness, Eliza lit a candle and went to the cupboard for a sheet of paper and a pen. She reached for the bottle of ink, but it was frozen, so she took up a pencil instead and sat at the table near the dying fire and began.

December 25, 1864
Dear Husband
On this most sacred of nights, I write to wish you a Happy Christmas & to tell you that your most welcome letter informing me the quilt had arrived, was joyously received. It was the best of all Christmas gifts. The children are overjoyed at their presents & I am warmed by your words that someday we will be together to share the quilt. Davy was busy with the knife, whittling a piece of wood which he said will become a stirring spoon for me. Luzena named the doll Miss Cat, for that ugly stray that got her tail caught in a reaper.

It has been a most unusual Christmas. At Post Office yesterday, Missouri Ann Stark that was Missouri Ann Martin received word her husband Hugh had been killed in battle. She had been abandoned to the Starks that misused her & wanted her to marry one-legged Edison, who is the most foul of creatures. On impulse, I asked her to live with me. She agreed to meet me at church today, but was followed by the Starks & a most unpleasant scene occurred in which Reverend Hamlin was threatened. But they were put in their place by the reverend, assisted by Print Ritter, the man who mended the wheel of our wagon last winter. Missouri Ann & Baby Nance are now asleep, even as I write this. I ask your approval for what I have done & would welcome any advice you can give me.

Eliza paused here. She gave a second thought about asking Will's advice, but she had nothing with which to erase the words. And with paper as scarce as it was, she did not wish to throw the sheet into the fire and begin again. She could always ignore Will's advice. It wouldn't be the first time. And if he complained, then she would tell him she had had to make the best of things as she saw them. After all, if he did not believe she could run the farm and make decisions in his stead, he should not have joined the army.

It was a beautiful Christmas day, the ground covered in white snow. I hitched Sabra to the sleigh & she carried us to church. I believe I saw a few looks of scorn at the undertaker's words on the sleigh & some few might have inquired of what we were thinking, but I also saw a glance or two of envy at such a handsome vehicle. When I told it about that you had traded the old wagon for the sleigh, there were murmurs of approval. Perhaps if I cannot make a success of the farm while you are away, I shall take up the new art of embalming.

Eliza frowned at what she had written. She hoped Will would understand she was only joking. But to be sure, she explained.

That is a little joke. Please excuse it. There is so little to laugh at these days.

Well, husband, we are well and snug here, our guests too, & lack only your presence to make this the merriest of Christmas days. We prayed at church for the welfare of all our men in the Union, as well as—

Eliza was about to say they had prayed for all soldiers, Union as well as Confederate, but she knew Will would not like that. So she crossed out "as well as" and continued.

—and asked the Lord to be with you in this noble cause. I myself prayed that the cause would soon conclude & I think others did, too, for many men from the country are away. Luzena said she had prayed for peace & a good dinner and was rewarded by half. I hope that you, too, had a Christmas feast.

Have a care for your safety, dear husband, & remember your little family at home that loves you & prays for you.

Your Affectionate Wife

Eliza A. Spooner

As she folded the letter to form its own envelope, she saw a damp spot on the paper and told herself it was a drop of water spilled at supper.

CHAPTER THREE

January 27, 1865

Snow had begun to fall, and Eliza tried to hurry Sabra by slapping the reins, but after a few quick steps, the old horse settled back into a walk. Wrapped in robes with her feet resting on a hot brick, Eliza was warm, even cozy, as she rode across the white road in the cutter, but she worried that the snow would make the drive home difficult. It couldn't be helped, she told herself. Sabra would go no faster, so Eliza nestled into the wool covers and looked out over the white landscape so like the one the day that she and Will had moved into the log house. There weren't many log houses. Most settlers lived in soddies, because trees were scarce. But Will had found land with a grove of trees on it, so they had built their second home out of logs, and the day they moved in, they were as proud of the house as if it had been a clapboard mansion. That memory warmed her, too.

The two of them along with the children had carried furniture and bedding, pots and kettles, books and china plates and silver teaspoons from the soddy into the new house. While Will placed the bed, the table and chairs, the clock they had brought from Ohio, Eliza arranged her pretty things—the silver teapot on a shelf in front of the white china platter with the blue feather edge. She put the tin candlesticks on the shelf, too, then changed her mind and set them on the table. She went outside and picked a bouquet of dried weeds and put them in her yellowware pitcher, which had been broken and mended with wire, and set the vase between the candlesticks. The arrange-ment was as pretty a picture as Eliza had ever seen.

When all was arranged to her satisfaction, Eliza made up the bed with homespun sheets and pillow slips edged with her own tatting, the blanket and quilts, then spread the prized Sunshine and Rain quilt over them. The quilt was taken out only on special occasions. It was her own design—she had named it, too—and she had made it for Will as a wedding present. With its indigo squares and red binding, it looked almost like a flag against the white stripes of chinking between the logs of the wall.

The Sunshine and Rain quilt was put away, but she would bring it out when Will came home, Eliza thought now. And they would hang his flag quilt on the wall.

The cabin wasn't large, but it was four times

the size of the soddy, and on that first night Luzena and Davy had played hide-and-seek in the great open space that served as kitchen, dining room, parlor, and bedroom for Eliza and Will. They had eaten supper, not much of a supper, just mush and milk, because Eliza had been too busy to prepare more, then had sat in front of the fire cracking black walnuts with a hammer and picking out the nutmeats. Luzena had fallen asleep in Eliza's lap, and Will had carried her up the ladder to the loft where she and Davy were to sleep. The boy had followed, remarking that the loft was as big as the soddy they had left.

They were tired and should have gone to bed, too, but Will and Eliza sat in the firelight, smiling at each other across the table, not having to say out loud how happy they were, for each knew the other was thinking just that.

"No wife ever had such a good provider," Eliza said at last.

"And no husband such a faithful wife." He reached across the table for her hand, and they sat like that for a moment, Eliza savoring the touch. Then Will looked toward the window, which was set with a rare pane of glass, and jumped up. "Look, dearest, it's snowing. Come and see."

They went to the door and stood there in the cold, looking out at the first winter snow, the flakes, big as ten-dollar gold pieces, floating down. In a few minutes, the snow coated the ground. Suddenly, Will grabbed Eliza's hand and pulled her out into the yard. He put his arms about her, and the two began to dance. They both loved to dance, had gone to every dance around when they were newly married, often not arriving home until morning light was creeping into the sky. Will guided her around the yard, twirling her about in the snow, until she did not know one direction from another. Oblivious to the falling flakes, they danced in the moonless dark until their clothes were soaked and then began to laugh at their foolishness. Will had kissed her long and hard, the kiss of a passionate man, then picked her up and carried her into the house. That dance was one of her precious moments, far too precious for Eliza to ever share with anyone else.

Now, Eliza relived that memory as she sat in the sleigh, putting her arms around herself as if Will were holding her, but her movement jerked the reins, and Sabra stopped. Eliza laughed at her foolishness and urged the horse forward again, wishing that Will really were beside her. But he would be. Maybe he would return home before winter was over. Surely he would be there by the next winter, to tell her again that the sleigh had not been necessary. He had joked about it in his first letter. Eliza had read the letter so many times that she had nearly memorized it. And now as she slid along the snowy road, she recalled the words.

September 22, 1864

Dearest Wife

We have fought a battle & there is no need to send the embalming sleigh just yet, for your husband is safe. I cannot say the same for many of our men or for the enemy. This is a cruel war & things are done by both the Rebs & us that were they known at home, would forever disgrace them. I think I do not need to tell you that I despise war almost as much as I do the Secesh for starting it. It warms my heart to know you are safe at home & that this war is a long way from you. I am glad you have little to worry about except the harvest.

We do not have a pretty time of it. We made coffee yesterday & discovered that each cupful had two or three boiled maggots in it. I foraged a real number one gooseberry pie. We are told not to jayhawk from the local people, but they are Rebs who would shoot us in the back if they could, so few soldiers do not help themselves when there is the opportunity. I myself take only a little. The pie was sitting on the table of a house whose occupants had run off to avoid the shooting, so I acquired it to keep it from going to waste. I believed it was the Lord's way of thanking us Yankee boys for our hard fighting. Others help themselves to whatever they find. One man foraged a mud lark or a slow deer, as a pig is called, a quart of salt, a sack full of potatoes & a Bible. I believe any Union soldier who steals a Bible needs it as much as a Southerner. Some of the Negroes here are as close to starvation as I ever saw, their backbones up against their breastbones. One woman begged an empty flour sack so she could use the leavings in it to make a soup for her child. I gave her the pie instead & you would think I had handed her a two-bit piece, so grateful was she. I am glad you do not have to see the suffering of these people. Their cruel treatment would be too much for you to imagine.

Eliza, I do not like this fighting. I believe I killed a man yesterday, shot him through the eye when he came at me shouting the dreadful Rebel yell. It is said the noise is like the call of a hyena. I cannot say, because I have never encountered the animal. But it puts such a fear into me as the time when I heard a panther scream. Such killing does not sit easy with me, although it is the job of all soldiers & he was only a Secesh. I hate these people even more for making me do the deed. The Bible tells us not to hate, but I believe the Lord did not know about Southerners when he set down His words.

Still, I hope that this war will be over & I will be home before planting. I never felt so lonesome for my wife & children before. You are the best of wives, Eliza, & I count myself the luckiest man in the world that you are home & safe from harm. I did not praise you often before, but I intend to do so more when I am home. And I will bring you a gold ring with a ruby in it.

    With love to our children, I remain
    Your Lonely Husband
    William T. Spooner

At last, the horse made it into town, and Eliza stopped the cutter in front of the store and tied the reins to the hitching post. She went inside, going directly to the stove to warm her hands. The store was deserted except for the shopkeeper, and Eliza was tempted to sit by the fire for a few minutes, but she must be on the road again before the storm worsened. So she went to the counter and took out the list of what she needed. Will had sent his pay in December and again in January, and Eliza was glad she had money to spend and wouldn't have to barter part of the crop. Now she could haggle over prices. The storekeeper took down a bag of flour and a sugar cone, molasses, salt, and the other items that Eliza needed. When he was finished and they had settled on the prices, he said, "I got a real nice wax doll her I could let you have for a good price for that little Stark girl living with you."

Eliza glanced at the doll and thought how much Nance would like it. Most likely, the man had ordered it for Christmas and failed to sell it. She remembered the toys in the store at Christmas Eve. The mothers had admired them, but like Eliza, they were hard up, with no spare cash to spend. So they had touched the tops and marbles and fingered the silk dress on the wax doll, but they had left her sitting on the counter. Eliza glanced at the doll, then shook her head.

"Didn't think so. Folks around here are too poor to buy hay for a nightmare." The man placed Eliza's purchases in her basket, and slung the bag of flour over his shoulder and started for the door.

"Is there mail?" Eliza asked.

The storekeeper, who was also the postmaster, stopped. "Almost forgot. There *is* a letter for you." He reached into one of the cubbyholes behind the counter and took out an envelope, hefted it, and dropped it into Eliza's basket. "I bet it's one of them valentines I heard about. I bet Will made you one. What do you say to that?"

Eliza colored at the suggestion, and the man, embarrassed that he had been so forward, went ahead of her out the door and placed the sack of flour under the sleigh robes where it wouldn't get wet. "You take care of yourself now, Miz Spooner. Ain't right for a lady to be out by herself in a storm, but what can you do when your man is away?" He untied the reins and handed them to Eliza, who had climbed into the sleigh and set her basket on the floor.

She had not expected a letter, had not thought to ask about one until the last minute, and she was tempted to open it right there in the sleigh. Maybe Will had indeed sent her a valentine. She'd read about them in *Peterson's Magazine*, although she had never seen one. But if she opened the envelope now, the contents would get wet. Besides, she should be on her way. And it would be more fun to open it at home in front of the fire, with the children beside her, just as she had the letter at Christmas. So Eliza settled back in the cold sleigh, warmed by the thought that there would be a letter and maybe even a valentine to read when she reached home.

The ride home was a slow one, and the gloom of the late winter afternoon had settled in by the time Eliza pulled into the barnyard. Davy came out to meet her and barn the horse and sleigh. "The road was slick, and Sabra took her time," Eliza explained.

"We were worried," Davy said, and Eliza thought he sounded just like Will when she had gone out and was late returning home.

Inside, Eliza found supper waiting. Missouri Ann had made biscuits and a kettle of soup. That young woman had been a blessing. How could

Eliza have hesitated even a minute before agreeing to take in Missouri Ann and Nance? Missouri Ann had done more than her share of cooking and washing, had helped keep up the house and care for the livestock. And most of all, she had been a companion to Eliza, who felt safer with her friend in the house. They had seen no more tramps, but they had found footprints in the snow. Eliza thought they belonged to vagrants, although she wondered if the Starks might have been about.

Luzena fetched slippers for her mother, telling Eliza to sit by the fire and warm her feet. Missouri Ann removed the basket from Eliza's arm and began putting away the contents. Then she held up the letter. "You got another letter?" she asked. She shook her head in wonder. "I never knew anybody that got two letters."

"It's from Will," Eliza replied. She turned to Luzena. "The storekeeper thinks it's a valentine."

"A what?" Missouri Ann asked, and Eliza laughed, explaining what a valentine was. "Sometimes they have lace pasted to them and colored paper, red, I think."

"Imagine that," Missouri Ann said. "If I had one of them, I'd put it in a picture frame and hang it on the wall."

"Of course, I don't know for sure that's what it is," Eliza said.

"Let's see, Mama. Open it," Luzena begged.

But Eliza replied they would wait until after supper so that she could read it aloud.

As they ate, both Eliza and Luzena glanced at the envelope that Missouri Ann had propped up on the mantel. After they were finished with the meal, Luzena cleared the dishes and brought the envelope to her mother, saying they had waited long enough. Nodding her approval, Eliza took the envelope and stared at the writing. The postmaster had slipped it into her basket, and this was the first time Eliza had seen the writing. The letter was big and twice the weight of Will's other letters, and it had been placed in a real envelope that was sealed on the flap with red wax. Eliza turned it over and stared at the handwriting again, realizing with a start that it was not familiar. "Oh," she said, disappointed. It had not even occurred to her that the letter might be from someone besides Will. "This is not from your father at all." At first, she was curious. Who could have sent her a letter? Then she felt a wave of apprehension, but she shook it off. Most likely, the letter was from one of her relatives. Of course, she thought, relieved. She broke the seal with her little finger, drew out the letter, and opened it. A second letter fell onto the table, facedown. Eliza let it lie there.

"Read it, Mama," Luzena said.

"Read it out loud," Davy added.

"Yes," Eliza said. She opened the folded piece

of paper and stared at it. "This is dated January 7, 1865."

"Read it," Missouri Ann said softly.

Eliza nodded. She took a deep breath and began.

January 7, 1865
Dear Mrs. Spooner
I trust you have been informed by now of the death of your husband, William Spooner—

Eliza dropped the paper as if it were on fire and gripped the edge of the table, looking up at Davy and Luzena, who were staring at her.

"Death?" Luzena asked. Her eyes were wide, and she gripped Nance's arm so hard that the child cried out.

"Death," Davy repeated.

Eliza put her hands over her eyes, then shook her head. Will wasn't dead, she thought. He couldn't be. Will had said he would come back. She needed him. They all needed him. He had promised he would be safe. Besides, she had received no official notification. Will's name had not been listed among the dead in the newspaper. "No, of course not. This is meant for someone else," she said.

She was not aware that Davy rose and put his hand on her shoulder, that Luzena moved beside her and took her hand. She looked up, glancing at each of them, even Baby Nance, and said, "It's a mistake. With all the men dying in battle, it happens all the time. Will is too good a man to lose. We need him." She paused. "Yes, it is a mistake."

"No, Mama," Davy said softly, the letter in his hand. "It's Papa. It says so right here. I'll read it."

Dear Mrs. Spooner
I trust by now—

Will skipped the rest of the sentence.

His death came on the day of December 21 in the second Battle of Saltville in Virginia, and by his sacrifice and God's grace, we won the fight. He died a hero's death, in the discharge of his duty. Just before he passed on, he asked to tell you he was happy to sacrifice his life for a noble cause.

It was the same sentiment contained in Missouri Ann's letter telling her of Hugh's death, Eliza thought, and she had not believed it about Hugh then, nor Will now. Will didn't want to die. He wanted to come home. He'd never said such a thing. Someone else had died, and they'd thought it was Will. That was it.

Your name was on his lips as he breathed his last.

I had the honor of serving as Billy's superior officer and knew him right well.

Not if you call him "Billy," Eliza thought.

There never was a better soldier or one who held his family more dear. Once, he told me after a battle where the air was so heavy with smoke you could barely see that he wished he was in a Kansas snowstorm, riding in his new sleigh.

Eliza gasped. Still, she couldn't accept the death. After all, there were other men from Kansas, other men who had sleighs.

The enclosed letter was discovered on your husband's person, and I believe he intended it be sent to you in case of his death. I have found that soldiers often write such letters before battle. I did not take the liberty of reading the letter, for I believe it may be intended for your eyes only.

Eliza reached for the letter on the table and turned it over, recognizing Will's handwriting. And then she knew. There had been no mistake. Will was dead. She started to cry and pressed the heels of her hands against her eyes to stop the tears, but they kept flowing.

"Why didn't the army tell you? Why wasn't it in the paper?" Davy asked, slapping his hand against the table, but Eliza could only shake her head.

Madam, you have the condolences of the President of the United States and the citizens of this country as well as myself. You have our thanks for your husband's part in this cause of liberty. Please know his death was not in vain.

I remain your servant
Randal S. Browne

They sat there stunned for a moment, even Baby Nance, who seemed to understand that something bad had happened. She crawled into her mother's lap, as Missouri Ann reached over and took Eliza's free hand. "I'm sorry. It ain't right. That man's said it true. Will Spooner was too good to die."

Eliza didn't hear her. Will was dead. She let the tears run down her face as she repeated it over and over to herself as if to accept the truth of it. She'd known from the day he joined the army that Will could be killed, but in her heart, she hadn't believed it possible.

"I wonder how many letters that man's had to write," Missouri Ann said, and Eliza realized that death wasn't hers alone. How many times had Randal S. Browne penned those same words to other widows? Will's death affected everyone—Mr. Browne, herself, the children. They needed her now, just as much as she needed Will. Eliza put her arms around Davy and Luzena and held them close.

Davy cussed under his breath, muttering, "Damn Secesh," while Luzena cried and asked who would care for them now.

"I will," Eliza said, realizing the awful burden that had been placed on her.

"You going to read Will's letter?" Missouri Ann asked.

"What?" Eliza had forgotten the missive that was enclosed in the envelope. Now she looked at the second letter, which lay on the table, folded up to form its own envelope. She picked it up and read her name, written in the handwriting she loved.

"Open it," Davy said.

Eliza started to unfold the paper, but then she stopped. "I couldn't. He must have had hours, maybe only minutes, to live when he wrote it. I couldn't stand to read his letter, knowing he was alive then and maybe only minutes later, he was dead. Maybe we'll read it later, but not now. I couldn't bear it."

She sat in the chair clutching the letter, while the others cleared the table and washed the dishes. After a time, Missouri Ann put Nance to bed.

"You go to bed, too," Missouri Ann told Davy and Luzena. "I'll sit with your ma."

The children, tired from grief, went up the ladder to the loft and were quiet except for sobs that broke the stillness from time to time.

"You want your Bible?" Missouri Ann asked. She reached for the leather volume on the mantel, near where the letter had rested.

Eliza shook her head. Her eyes were too tired to read. Besides, what words of comfort were in the Bible that she didn't already know? What comfort could any words give her now?

"Get you on your night dress then," Missouri Ann, said, helping Eliza to stand. "Raise up your arms." Eliza let her friend undress her and slip the white cotton shift over her. Then Missouri Ann went to the trunk and took out Eliza's Sunshine and Rain quilt and wrapped her in it. She blew out the candles, and now, only the dying fire lit the room.

"I'll sit for a moment. You go to bed," Eliza said, still clutching Will's letter. She sat down in the rocker, the one Will had made for her when she was expecting Davy.

Missouri Ann started to protest, but it was clear that in her sorrow, Eliza wanted to be alone. So Missouri Ann lay down on her side of the bed, and after a time, her breath slowed in sleep.

Eliza rocked back and forth in a rhythm that ought to have made her sleepy. But she was wide awake, tears silently rolling down her face. Will had been dead more than a month. She had done the milking, had fixed supper, had fed the animals and quilted with Missouri Ann, and all that time Will was dead. They had celebrated Christmas, had read his letter, and Will was dead. Each time she'd heard a horse in the lane, she had half expected the rider to be Will, home from the war, but Will was in his grave. Would she ever know where it was, or would his resting place go unmarked? He wouldn't even be buried on the farm he loved, where she could erect a stone and tend the mound of dirt over his coffin. She remembered the Christmas letter and how happy Will had been with the quilt. Was it now his shroud? Would he wear it for all eternity? Or had it been left to rot in the mud of the battlefield?

Eliza rocked a long time, thinking of Will, of herself, of the children. The fire was dead when she rose, opened the door, and looked out at the snow. It had fallen all day and been swept into white drifts by the wind. But the wind had stopped, and the snow fell straight down. Another time, she would have found the night magical, but now she could only wonder about Will far away, lying under a blanket of white. He had died in Virginia, the letter said. Eliza tried to think where that was. Did it snow in Virginia? Maybe there was rain, a hard wild rain that washed away the dirt over his grave.

Will had loved the snow, the cleanness of it, the quiet, the sense of peace it brought, had loved it even though winter meant hard chores. Eliza was not aware of the cold as she stepped outside, one hand clutching Will's letter, the other raised to catch the falling flakes. They covered her hand and the white night dress as she stepped off the porch. She remembered how Will had looked when he came in from the barn in a snowstorm, the pale flakes on his dark hair, his face cold as he hugged her against him, savoring her warmth. She remembered he'd once tied a rope between the house and the barn so that he wouldn't get lost in a blizzard. Eliza thought about death in that pure white cold, a cleansing death. She would simply go to sleep and never wake. She remembered something else, too.

Eliza moved into the yard and raised her head, as if she were looking up at Will. Then slowly, she took a step forward, raised her arms, and began to dance.

CHAPTER FOUR

March 31, 1865

"My, such pretty pieces and perfectly put together," Ettie Espy observed, running her hand over the quilt top. The five women were seated around Eliza's quilt frame, stitching on a top that she and Missouri Ann had pieced during the winter.

Missouri Ann had found the cut out pieces after they learned of Will's death and taken them out and given them to Eliza, saying quilting would help her with her sorrow. Eliza had worked on her sewing as if by rote, stitching together the pieces that Missouri Ann laid out for her. Her tears had dropped onto the fabric strips, as she realized Will would never sleep under one of her quilts again. She used the half-finished top to wipe her eyes, then Missouri Ann took it from her and ironed the damp places between her fingers. Eliza wondered how Missouri Ann could be so much more accepting of her own husband's death, but maybe the girl was just grateful to be away from the Starks.

Although it was only March, the women had moved the frame outside so that they could sit in the shade of the apple trees that were budding in the orchard. The light was better there, and they could pretend to smell blossoms, a scent that meant spring after a long and lonely winter. Not that the women weren't aware that it was spring. In fact, they should have been planting and tending to other duties on their farms, but they had taken a break for a day. The five called themselves "war widows," although only Eliza, Missouri Ann, and Mercy Eagles had lost their men. The husbands of the other two were off fighting the war, and the women had been left behind to care for farms and children. Farming was hard enough with the men at home, but it was time-consuming, backbreaking work for women with only their children to help them—and all their normal household duties to attend to. Nonetheless, they had plowed and planted, sometimes joining forces to help each other, for there were no men to hire and no money to pay them even if they could be found. The women should have been attending to farm duties that day, but they had decided just after Christmas that they would meet one day each month, no matter how wasteful of their time it might seem, to share their lives over the quilt frame. At first, she had refused to attend the quiltings, saying she was in mourning, but the others had insisted.

Now, Eliza was grateful her friends were there, would make her put away her sorrow for a few hours. Because of them, she might go five or ten minutes without thinking about Will.

Four of the five had quilted together for years. They thought to put aside sewing bees when their husbands joined the Union army but decided they needed the day with each other. Talking about fears and hardships made them realize they were not alone in their troubles. Telling each other about their small joys—the letters from the camps and battlefields, the triumphs of their children, the first shoots sprouting from the seeds—made such pleasures seem even more important. And when the news came that husbands had died, the new widows were sustained by the love and support of the others. "How could I cope with this war without my quilting friends," Mercy Eagles had said, and the others had nodded their agreement.

Besides, the quilts were being stitched for an Independence Day celebration, where they would be auctioned off for the benefit of the soldiers. "Nobody could fault a widow for spending one day a month working for war relief," Mercy had told Eliza.

The gatherings refreshed them, and for Eliza, they brought a sense of normalcy for a few hours. She would savor a remark and think she would repeat it to Will. Or she would ask for a recipe, because Will would like the dish. And she would smile as if Will were still alive, before realizing she would never confide in Will or sit with him over dinner again.

For all of the women, the quiltings became the highlight of each month. They looked forward to the gatherings, each bringing food to share and children, of course. The little ones were romping through the orchard just then, playing war with sticks for guns.

"Eliza, you are indeed the best stitcher in Wabaunsee County," Ettie announced in her strong voice.

Eliza was deep in thought, and a moment passed before she realized Ettie was talking to her. "Oh, but those stars are not mine," Eliza protested. "Missouri Ann made them."

The women turned to Missouri Ann, who blushed and bent over her needle in embarrassment at the attention.

"I suppose that's the best compliment a body could give you, mistaking your work for Eliza's," Anna Bean told Missouri Ann.

As the others nodded, Ettie exchanged a glance with Mercy Eagles. The women had not been happy when Eliza announced that she could no longer be part of the group unless Missouri Ann was included.

"But she will spoil our little friendship," Mercy had said. "We've quilted together for years and never felt the need to bring in anyone else."

"Four is a perfect number for a quilt frame. Five will set us off our pace," Anna Bean had added.

"Besides, she's a Stark," Ettie had reminded Eliza.

"Only by marriage, and you know yourself, because you were at church on Christmas Day, how she escaped from those people. She has been a great help on the farm. I can't imagine how I got along without her. She's very like a sister to me now," Eliza told them. "Besides, she lives with me. How can I ask her to stay to herself while the four of us stitch?" The conversation had taken place before Will's death, and Eliza was glad she had insisted on Missouri Ann becoming part of the group. Without her friend, Eliza could not have made it through those first dark days of death.

Because they were generally kind women, the others had not been able to answer.

After just a single day of sewing, the women had accepted Missouri Ann as one of them. "She's fast and her stitches are small," Ettie observed. At more than fifty, she was the oldest of the group—and the largest, taller by two inches than Eliza and weightier by half. Some thought she was frosty-nosed, but her friends knew her to be a kind woman who would share her last potato. Her husband had been one of the first to join up, and later, two sons had enlisted. One of them had been killed at Shiloh.

"And when Missouri Ann opens her mouth, she has something interesting to say," Anna said, sending a sly glance at Ettie, who was known to gnaw a subject to death, just as a dog would a bone.

"I believe she fits, and she's a worker," Mercy added, and that had settled it. Calling a Kansas woman a worker was the best compliment anyone could pay her.

Now the women stopped to admire the stars Missouri Ann had made for the quilt. It was a Log Cabin, a much-loved design because a few of the first homes in the county had been log cabins, Eliza had explained to Missouri Ann when she chose the pattern.

"Is there a Soddy quilt?" Missouri Ann had asked.

"It would have to be all browns and dirty."

Eliza and Missouri Ann pieced the Log Cabin squares using scraps of red for the centers, because red represented the hearth, the center of the home. They placed a series of dark strips along two adjacent sides of the red squares, and light strips on the other two sides. Then they stitched the finished squares together to make a second pattern, called "Barn Raising." The quilt was a pattern within a pattern. What made the quilt different from other Log Cabins were the white stars that Missouri Ann cut out and appliquéd to each red center before the "logs" were added around the sides. She cut the stars without a pattern. Some were lopsided, the legs unequal, and the sizes varied. But the quilters were charmed by the variety. They spent several minutes deciding whether to quilt an outline around the stars or to make an X through the red square. They decided on the latter, perhaps because the stitching would go quicker.

"I never saw a thing so pretty. Why, with this quilt over you, you'd know you were sleeping under the sky," Anna said. She was a little thing, not more than a few years over twenty, with the blue eyes and yellow hair of a china doll. Eliza was amazed that such a delicate woman could work so hard. Anna had always been fashionably dressed, with clothes she made herself and wore over hoops, and her children were as spotless as children could be. When Eliza had first seen the Beans' little stone house, she'd thought it looked like a drawing from *Peterson's Magazine*, with its antimacassars and a paisley shawl draped over the love seat, the vase of beaded flowers, an arrangement of dried grasses. Now Anna did the plowing and planting, too. Eliza noticed that Anna's dress was frayed, and the sleeve soiled, the jacket loose. The woman was barefoot, as well, although she still wore hoops. The war had taken its toll on her, but then what woman whose husband had gone to war hadn't suffered? At least her husband was still alive, Eliza thought, then bit her lip. She would not let herself think "what if"—what if Anna's husband had died instead of Will. She would be glad that Cosby Bean was still alive.

"I believe I'd like to make a quilt like this with stars, a good quilt that I could pass down to my daughter and granddaughter so's they'd remember Cosby fought to save the nation," Anna continued.

"You think someday our granddaughters will sit like this over a quilt frame, maybe right here in Wabaunsee County, Kansas?" Mercy asked.

"I hope it won't be in wartime," Eliza said. "I'd rather think of them stitching in happier days, without any worries—and without any slaves to be freed." Or husbands dead on a battlefield, she thought. She hoped their granddaughters would not know such sorrow.

"Cosby doesn't approve of slavery, but he didn't join up to free the slaves. He's fighting to preserve the Union," Anna said.

"It's the same thing, ain't it?" Missouri Ann asked. She had taken eight tiny stitches on her needle and pulled it through the quilt, making sure each stitch was tight.

"It is, and it isn't," Ettie explained, glancing at Missouri Ann's stitches, then nodding her approval. As the most outspoken woman in the group, Ettie liked to preside over discussions, and the others generally yielded to her, because she was considered a deep thinker.

The women were silent, until Eliza said, "Well, what of it is and what of it isn't?"

Ettie paused to make a tiny knot that was all but invisible, and snip off her thread. She removed the inch left in her needle and tossed it onto the ground "for a bird's nest," she said. Then she cut a length of thread, put it through her needle, secured the end in the quilt, and began stitching again. "It was slavery that caused the South to secede, and the North went to war to keep them from doing it. But you've seen how some of the Union supporters here treat our free Negroes, like Andy Jones that works for Print Ritter. I think they would rather throw food to the pigs than give it to a starving colored man."

"I think some of the men's gone off to the war to have a good time," Missouri Ann said. She blushed when she saw the others had stopped stitching and were staring at her, as if they wondered whether that had been Hugh's reason for joining up.

"I suppose that's so," Eliza said, thinking that was exactly why Missouri Ann's husband went for a soldier.

"Hugh went to save the Union," Missouri Ann said quickly.

"Then why didn't the other Starks join?" Ettie asked.

"I couldn't rightly say," Missouri Ann replied.

"Because they're copperheads," Davy interjected. The women had not seen him standing near them, and they paused.

Eliza admonished him, saying he should keep such thoughts to himself unless asked. She shooed him away with her hand.

"I heard her say it," the boy insisted. He pointed his stick gun at Missouri Ann. "A copperhead's almost as bad as a Secesh."

"Mrs. Stark is our friend and guest, and you will not say another word. The idea!" Eliza glanced around the circle and shook her head. "Davy hates the Johnnies because they killed Will. That's what causes him to say such things."

"But it's true," Missouri Ann told the women. "Hugh was different, but the rest of the Starks, they don't like Negroes any more than a yellow dog. Dad Stark said a black man that's freed, well, you might as well shoot him, for all he's worth."

Eliza drew her arms to her sides and didn't look up. She wondered if Missouri Ann felt the same way as the Starks. They'd never talked about it.

It was Mercy, her needle poised over the quilt, who asked Missouri Ann if she agreed.

"No, ma'am, I do not. Dad Stark said they're dumb enough to drown in a pitcher of water, but I knowed free Negroes that was smarter than some with the name of Stark. When I growed up, my pa was a follower of John Brown. He said John Brown was a saint of the Lord."

"Amen," said Ettie. "It looks like we're all against slavery."

"Well, if we aren't, why are we quilting for the Union?" Eliza asked.

"I don't care a peach pit for black folks," Mercy said, her dark eyes flashing. "If it wasn't for them, Nathaniel would be alive." Mercy had not lived in Wabaunsee County as long as the others. She had moved there only four years earlier with her husband and two daughters, who were now eight and twelve. Eliza had met her in the post office and had been taken with her right off. Who wouldn't have been? She was so vivacious that Eliza hadn't realized until later that Mercy was plain-looking, of average height, with black hair parted in the middle and pulled tightly behind her ears into a knot. Her clothes had been unremarkable, severe dark browns, but they set off Mercy's bright face and dancing eyes. When Mercy announced she loved to quilt, Eliza, without asking Anna and Ettie, had asked her to join their group.

Now Eliza, shocked at her friend's words, looked up from her stitching. "Surely you don't blame the Negroes for the war."

"And why not? If the coloreds hadn't come to America, they wouldn't be slaves, and if there weren't any slaves, there wouldn't be a war."

"But they couldn't help it," Ettie said. "They didn't choose to be slaves. They got snatched up out of Africa and brought here and sold."

"Maybe they should have killed themselves then. All's I'm saying is I don't want them in Wabaunsee County. I'd as soon shoot one as let him on my farm." She paused and added, "I never thought slavery was such a bad thing. I'm surprised you don't hate those people, too, Eliza. Will would be alive if it wasn't for them."

For a moment, Eliza couldn't think of how to reply. She wished Will hadn't been killed, wished it more than anything in the world, but she blamed the South, not the Negroes. "You think it's all right to own slaves?" she asked at last.

Mercy shrugged. "They get plenty to eat and a place to sleep and don't have to pay taxes."

"They don't own land," Ettie told her.

"I say it's not such a bad life. Maybe it's the natural order of things."

"Well, I say God's no more in favor of slavery in America than He was of slavery in Egypt," Eliza said, catching her thread as she pulled her needle through the quilt, causing it to knot. She picked at the knot with her needle, her head bowed to hide the tears that had formed in her eyes. The sudden mention of Will's name did that to her. She stared at the quilt, while she blinked back the tears, thinking of her husband lying under the Christmas quilt for only a few nights. She wondered what had happened to it.

"The slaves in Egypt were Jews, just like the postmaster in town, not colored people," Mercy said. "I wouldn't be in favor of selling the postmaster into slavery."

"Who'd buy him?" Missouri Ann muttered, then covered her mouth with her hand as if she shouldn't have spoken. The others burst out laughing, which diffused the tension.

But Ettie wouldn't let things lie. She said that although President Lincoln had freed the slaves, she'd heard there were slave catchers who kidnapped free Negroes in the North and took them South to sell. She turned to Missouri Ann. "And I heard Dad Stark is one of them."

Missouri Ann looked up and found the others staring at her. She shrugged. "I wouldn't know for sure, but I heard Dad Stark say they ought to snatch up Andy Jones and sell him down South."

"But Andy's been free ever since I've been in Kansas. The idea!" Ettie said, jamming her needle into the quilt with such force that she pricked her finger. "Now look what I've done. I've bled on your quilt, Eliza."

"Oh, one drop won't hurt it. After all, this is *bleeding* Kansas," Eliza replied, smiling just a little. Then she asked Ettie if she were saying that once an escaped slave reached Kansas, he wasn't safe, even though Mr. Lincoln had set him free, that he could be captured and sent back to his owner?

"I am. As long as there's money in it, there are men who'll work for the devil," Ettie replied.

"Maybe that would keep those colored people out of Wabaunsee County," Mercy said.

"Why, I'd think you might want to hire them to help you in your fields now that your husband isn't coming back," Anna told her. "I've heard they're hard workers, and cheap."

"Not me. I'd shoot any of them that came on my farm," Mercy replied.

"You already said that. And I heard you said it in town, too. I did not think you were a vengeful woman. You were given the wrong name," Ettie said. "If one of those coloreds came to *my* farm, I'd invite him in for supper and give him a rhubarb pie."

Mercy bristled and was about to reply, when Eliza spoke up. "I don't think we have to worry about anybody snatching up Negroes now, what with the war almost done." She paused, then looked up at the sun and asked where the time had gone. It was long past the dinner hour, she said. No wonder the children were fighting a battle out there. She asked Mercy to help her set out the food. Eliza stuck her needle into the quilt and stood up, stretching her back. She ached not just from bending over the quilt frame but from the farm work, too.

"They don't understand what it's like to lose a husband," Mercy told Eliza as the two headed for the house. "There's an awfulness to it. You and me and Missouri Ann, we know."

Eliza reached for her friend's hand and squeezed it, letting the touch warm her. "We need each other, Mercy. There is indeed an awfulness to being alone."

The dinner was a simple one, but it was better than what the women and children generally ate. Eliza had added potatoes and turnips and onions to stretch the chicken stew. The pie Ettie brought was made with molasses instead of sugar, while Mercy's cake was sweetened with applesauce. But there was cream to pour over the desserts, because the women still had cows to milk.

Eliza blessed the dinner and asked for victory for the North, and then, her voice trembling, she prayed for the safe return of Ettie's and Anna's men. The women helped the children, thinking if the dinner were sparse, they would rather go without than let the little ones be hungry. But there was more than enough, and once the children were served, the women dished up for themselves. They sat in the sunlight and ate slowly, hoping they felt full before the food was gone.

Eliza did not want to revisit the subject of slavery. Nor did she want to talk again about the war dead for fear she would cry. So she brought up the Independence Day fair. How much did they think the Log Cabin quilt would bring? she asked the others.

Mercy guessed seven dollars, and Ettie said it would more likely be four.

"But it's as nice a quilt as was ever made. Surely it's worth more than four," Mercy said. The women had set aside their plates and returned to quilting.

It didn't matter what it was worth, Eliza told her. It was what somebody would give for it, and there wasn't much cash around. Many people were barely making it. She didn't add that without Will's pay, she was one of them.

Then it seemed like a waste of their time to stitch the quilt, Mercy observed.

Anything was worthwhile if it was for the soldiers, Anna told her.

"Sewing seems a poor way to win a war," Ettie said.

"We are women," Anna replied. "We stay at home. We don't do the fighting."

Ettie took a few stitches, then looked across the orchard. "Oh, to see and be in it all. Wouldn't that be something?"

"Well, I for one would think it unladylike to shoulder a gun," Anna argued.

"Oh, bosh, Anna," Ettie said, pulling her needle through the quilt so hard that she broke the thread. "Now look what I've done."

"Nathaniel believed a woman was an ornament of the home. I want a man to take care of me," Mercy insisted.

Ettie leaned over and licked the end of the thread still stuck in the quilt, then put the end through her needle. "A mighty fine job Nathaniel's done of that, him dead and buried."

"Ettie! How could you?" Eliza reprimanded. She leaned back on the stump that she used for a chair, feeling as hurt as Mercy must be. How dare Ettie suggest the death of their two husbands was their fault! Then she glanced at Missouri Ann. Eliza had almost forgotten that she, too, had lost her husband. But Missouri Ann seemed to accept widowhood better than Mercy and Eliza. Or perhaps she was just grateful to be on Eliza's farm.

"Well . . ." Ettie glanced shame-faced at the other women. "I shouldn't have said it, and I beg your pardon, Mercy, but I ask you who's to care for the women when their men are killed in this war? You can't raise two daughters on Nathaniel's pension. Nor can Eliza or Missouri Ann, or the others. It seems there's a vacant chair in every house in Wabaunsee County."

Eliza spoke up. "Sometimes I wish *I* were fighting the South. To be idle in time of war is torture."

"Oh, we're not idle," Ettie told her. "Just look around this sewing circle. Everyone has a

101

needle." She paused while the women looked at each other. "It's just that I feel useless with nothing more to stop the war than stitch a quilt. I wish we could do something that made a real difference."

"What?" Anna asked.

"That's just it. What? We're women. What can we do?" Ettie asked.

The quilters grew silent. The afternoon was drowsy. It was only March, but the sun was warm, and there was just a little breeze blowing through the trees. Eliza wiped her fingers on her skirt, since her hands had begun to perspire. She found it hard to push her needle through the quilt because it was damp from the moisture on her hands. She glanced around at the others and saw that they, too, had grown listless. Their quilting had slowed. So Eliza suggested they take a break and have a dipper of water. She stood up and wriggled her back to get out the kinks. The others seemed eager to stop and stood, too. Anna lifted her arms in a stretch, and Eliza saw the woman's jacket rise and her skirt go taut over her stomach and realized her friend was pregnant. She must have conceived just before her husband left in the fall.

Anna caught Eliza's glance and said, "June, probably. I'm not sure."

The other women had gone to the well and were dipping water from the bucket. Eliza put her arm around Anna. Summer was the best time to have a baby, she said, although both knew summer was also a difficult time for a farm woman to give birth, especially a woman who was tending a farm by herself. "You'll find someone to help with the crops," Eliza said.

"The crops!" Anna cried. "What do I care about crops? It's bearing a child alone that scares me. What if something should happen to me? What would become of the babies? Who's to care for them?" Anna had two boys, the oldest only three.

"You've gone through childbirth before."

"But not without Cosby. Oh, Eliza, I can't sleep for fear of what might happen. I did not want to get this way with Cosby going off to war. I told Cosby I did not . . ." Her voice trailed off, then she added, "But we love each other so. What will I do?"

Anna's mother would always take them, Eliza replied.

Her friend put her hands to her face. "That's just it. Mother is with child herself. It was the saddest day of my life when she told me that she, too, would have another baby."

"At her age?"

"She is forty-seven. I was her first, born when she was sixteen. She has been bearing children for two thirds of her life! Eight births so far, and I do not know how many other times she conceived and lost the half-made babies. It is too much for her."

Eliza tried to think of something comforting to say but could not. She was grateful Will had not left her in that condition.

"I had thought when I found out that at least I would have Mother to help. After all, my youngest brother is seven. And not knowing I myself was in the same condition, Mother thought I would come to her aid. It is a conundrum of the worst sort."

"Perhaps the men will be home by then." Eliza thought of the stupidity of her words and added, "Perhaps the sun will rise in the west." She laughed but not with humor.

"I suppose I will just have to manage. I did not think I could run the farm without Cosby, but I have done a decent job of it."

They all had, Eliza replied. And Anna would do a decent job of birthing that baby, she added.

"I must carry on alone. There is nothing else that can be done."

Eliza smiled at her friend. "You can't prevent having the baby, and you have done all right with that in the past. You may not have Cosby, but you'll have us, Anna. We'll see you through it. Maybe that's what women can do in wartime. They can care for each other when their men cannot care for them." She grasped her friend's hand as she thought perhaps that was not much of a challenge. And then she had a terrible thought. What if Anna's husband, too, did not come home? Three of the five women had already lost their husbands. Eliza could not bear the thought that Cosby Bean, too, might die.

Both Eliza and Anna were distraught as they returned to the quilt frame. The others did not seem to notice, however, for they were silent, too, lost in their own thoughts. They continued to stitch, talking only to ask for the scissors or the thread or whether it was time to roll the finished section of quilt over the end of the frame to expose the unstitched portion. Every now and then one of the women stood up to stretch her back or to check on a child who was whining or who had grown too quiet. Mercy seemed shocked when one of her daughters, who was playing soldier, complained, "Why do I have to be the damn Reb all the time?"

"Such cussing. I don't know where she picked it up," Mercy said, getting up from the frame to reprimand the girl.

"Probably from her father," Ettie told the others when Mercy was out of earshot.

"Ettie, he is dead!" Anna said, shocked.

"Even more reason for her to cuss," Ettie replied, and Eliza couldn't help smiling. She wondered again about laughter in the midst of the deepest grief.

There were chores to do, and the quilters were anxious to be on their way. They stitched quickly, and by late afternoon, they had finished the quilt. All that remained was to roll the backing over the front of the quilt to form a binding, and Eliza would do that later. She unrolled the quilt from the frame, and she and Missouri Ann held it up, as the others admired it.

"I must have worked on a thousand quilts, but I never see a finished one that doesn't take away my breath," Ettie said. "Missouri Ann, those stars look like they fell out of the sky."

Missouri Ann sucked in her breath with pride. Then she and Eliza folded the quilt and rested it on the frame. The others gathered their children, along with their dishes and needles and scissors.

Just as the women finished, two men, one on horseback, the other driving a wagon, came into the barnyard. There was a bend in the lane to the Spooner farmhouse, so the men could not have known the women were gathered in the orchard, and they appeared surprised to see so many.

"Why, we are intruding," John Hamlin said, taking off his hat and greeting the women.

"Not so's you'd notice. We were just leaving," Ettie said, but she made no move for her buggy.

Eliza went up to the men and told them to get down and help themselves to the well water. John exchanged a glance with the second man, Print Ritter, and both dismounted, leading their horses to the water trough, then going on toward the well.

"I was on my way to town and stopped to see if you had need of anything, Mrs. Spooner," John said.

John Hamlin had been kind, had stopped to give his condolences and ask if there was wood he could chop or harnesses to mend. Still, the Spooner farm was hardly on his way to town. The women must have realized that, too, and now they were in no hurry to leave. They stared as the two men headed for the well, but then Print stopped in front of Missouri Ann and nodded. "How do, Mrs. Missouri Ann," he said, touching the brim of his hat.

Anna and Mercy exchanged a knowing glance, and Eliza looked away to keep from smiling. It wasn't the first time the blacksmith had found a reason to stop at the Spooner farm and engage Missouri Ann in conversation.

Ettie opened her mouth, then shut it and climbed into her buggy. "I'll see you in church," she said, flicking the reins across her horse's back and starting down the road. Anna followed, with Mercy at her side, knitting needles out and working furiously, for she was one to always knit socks or scarves or mittens for the soldiers. The two grinned at Missouri Ann, whose face was red with embarrassment.

Eliza hoped the women would not tease

Missouri Ann later. She had known the first time Print Ritter called, using some excuse about just passing by and offering to have a look at Eliza's wagon wheel, which he'd noticed had begun to wobble, that he had taken an interest in her friend.

But there was not time for visiting that day. She and Missouri Ann had chores to do and supper to be gotten, and she hoped the men would not stay long. She had had enough company for a while.

John and Print went to the well, taking their time with the water, waiting until the dust from the departing vehicles settled, to return to the women. The men's faces were serious, and Eliza realized that this was not a courting visit.

"We have need of your help," John told Eliza, glancing at Missouri Ann as if he were not sure she should be included in the conversation.

"You can trust Mrs. Missouri Ann," Print assured him. "Mrs. Spooner would be of no use if Mrs. Missouri Ann wasn't in on it."

John looked at Missouri Ann out of the corner of his eye, then nodded and turned to Eliza. "I speak of a matter of grave importance—and great secrecy. We men may fight the battles." He stopped and glanced at his arm where a bone had been shattered by a bullet. Both men had been wounded in the war and been discharged. "We may fight the battles," he repeated, "but you women, too, must be part of the business of keeping our country free. I'm afraid I must challenge you to do something dangerous, but I think you will not turn me down, because you will do what is necessary to win the war for the Union, for the cause for which your husbands died."

CHAPTER FIVE

March 31, 1865

Eliza pressed her palms together, fingers pointed upward, as if she were praying, but she was not. She was remembering how the women had wished that there were a way they could do more than stitch for the war effort, more than wait and suffer. She herself had expressed the desire to join the fighting. Now, it seemed that John Hamlin was about to bring her a challenge, and Eliza wondered if she would be up to it. She leaned forward, anxious, and nodded at him to continue.

John looked at Missouri Ann again, stared at her for a long time, until Print shrugged and said, "I'd be happy to do the milking, Mrs. Missouri Ann, if you'd accompany me to the barn."

The men's intention was obvious. John wanted to talk to Eliza alone. Despite what Print had said, John didn't trust Missouri Ann. Eliza spoke up. "No need. Davy will tend to the milking and is in the barn already. Anything you have to say to me can be said in front of Mrs. Stark. She is as

110

loyal a Unionist as I am. Both of our husbands died for the cause."

"She is a Stark," John reminded Eliza.

"Have you forgotten how you yourself helped her to escape from those foul people on Christmas Day?"

John considered that. "Have they been a-bothering you since then, the Starks?"

Eliza shrugged. Part of a fence had been torn down, and there was a hole in the henhouse where a fox had gotten in. The two women had returned home from town one afternoon to discover large rocks blocking the lane. And then there were the tracks in the snow. But Eliza hadn't actually seen the Starks, so she couldn't say for sure that this had been their mischief.

"Not that we can prove," Eliza replied. "If they've been here, it hasn't been often, and we haven't seen them."

"You are alone now?" John asked.

Except for the children, Eliza told him. Luzena had taken Nance into the house.

John nodded, satisfied. He moved closer to the two women and lowered his voice. "There is an escaped slave who needs to be hidden. She is only passing through, but she is ill and needs a place of safety until she is well enough to go on. I am asking you to provide it."

"The poor thing," Eliza gasped. "I am so sorry for her."

"Mrs. Espy told us about the men that captures Negroes and takes them South to be sold, but why's anyone want to steal a sick woman?" Missouri Ann asked. "Besides, the war seems 'bout over. Who'd buy a slave now? Makes no sense to me."

"She is not an ordinary slave." John looked around, as if thinking someone might have crept up on them and was listening. They were alone. Still, he lowered his voice. "She killed her mistress. Her owner wants her back so he can punish her."

"Oh!" Eliza took a deep breath. Caring for an escaped slave was one thing, but bringing a murderer onto the farm—and one whose victim was a woman—was something else. What if the woman was depraved? She might hate all white people and turn on her or Missouri Ann, or one of the children. No matter how sympathetic she was at the colored woman's plight, Eliza couldn't allow her to live with them. "Mr. Hamlin, I'm sorry—" she began, but John didn't let her finish.

"She was beaten by her mistress, and when the woman wasn't satisfied with the welts she'd caused on the slave's back, she poured salt into the wounds. And then she turned on the slave's son and whipped him to death."

Eliza and Missouri Ann stared at John in horror. "What had she done?" Eliza asked.

"Stolen a teaspoon of sugar for her boy. The

woman beat the slave for taking the sugar, then turned on the boy for eating it."

"How old was he?" Missouri Ann asked.

"Not yet three."

"She beat a baby to death? The monster!" Eliza cried.

"The boy's father was the master—the mistress's own husband." John paused, then added, "You must forgive me, ladies, for speaking of such an indelicacy, but in times like these, frankness is called for. It is not unusual for a master to father the children of young slave women. The man refused to interfere when his own son was beaten, so Sukey—that is the slave's name—grabbed the whip, thinking to stop the outrage, and struck her mistress such a blow that it broke her skull. In the South, the punishment for striking a white person is severe; the penalty for killing one is death. With her very life at stake, Sukey ran off, and has made her way to Kansas. Lord knows how she got this far in her condition. We used to send the escaped slaves north to Canada, but that is the obvious route. I think we will send Sukey west to Colorado when she is well enough to travel."

"The little boy?" Eliza said.

"He was dead before Sukey took the whip, most likely put into the earth without a marker. But God will know where he is."

Eliza and Missouri Ann both bowed their

heads. "Killing her mistress might be thought retribution," Eliza said.

"In the North, yes. But in the South, it is greeted with outrage. A white person's life is not worth that of two Negroes—or a hundred, for that matter. The owner has offered a substantial reward for the return of Sukey, and it is known she has come this way. If she is turned over to her former master, she will be hanged or maybe torn apart by dogs. There are other slow means of death that are as bad. She would die by inches."

Eliza nodded understanding. "Our Union law should protect her here in Kansas, but as we have been told, there are men who would capture a slave and take her south."

"Men like Dad Stark," Missouri Ann added.

"Men like Dad Stark," John repeated. "And his sons." He thought that over and said, "I beg your pardon again, Mrs. Missouri Ann. I should not have spoken ill of your family."

"They're not my family no more. Besides, my husband wasn't like the others," Missouri Ann replied. "I know the Starks better than anybody. They'd sell their own for a Yankee dollar."

"Why do you want to bring Sukey here?" Eliza asked. She was sure from the rumors that John Hamlin had helped slaves escape, that he was a stop on the Underground Railroad. Surely he had better places to hide a colored woman than on the Spooner farm. "It is said you have hidden many on your own land. Why bring her to us?"

"For that very reason, that it is known I've aided other contraband. My farm is the first place the Starks or any others would look for her. And there *will* be others. The offer of a reward will bring out the old slave catchers. As you know, there are many in the state who are sympathetic toward the South and do not oppose slavery," John replied. "Print has offered to hide her in the smithy, but he, too, has hidden slaves in the past and would be under suspicion."

"*You* done that, Mr. Ritter?" Missouri Ann said, a sense of awe in her voice. "I never heard of nothing so brave. Why, the Starks is at the smithy every week. You sure did fool them."

Print blushed.

"We believe the Starks watch us. This would be the worst place to hide an escaped slave," Eliza said. "They would spot her right away."

John shook his head. "That makes your farm the best of hiding places, as long as you confine Sukey to the house. The Starks are in town now. Since they keep such close watch on you, they will have not the slightest suspicion Sukey was sneaked into your house during their absence. As they have been warned to stay away, they have no call to come into your house, or even your barnyard. They will never know she is here. Your farm will be the perfect hiding place."

"They think I hate the coloreds as much as they do," Missouri Ann said. "I was never brave enough to say my mind."

"Then indeed this is the perfect place. It will be for only a few days. Sukey is too exhausted and too sick yet from the whipping to travel farther. It is a wonder she made it all the way from Louisiana. Poor thing, she traveled by night and hid in trees and ditches, until by luck, she was found by one of our people—a "conductor" on the Underground Railroad. Then she was sent north hidden in wagons and carts. She has great courage, and I believe you will like her. What do you say, Mrs. Spooner?" John asked.

Eliza turned away to think. Hiding the woman for a night or maybe two was one thing, but keeping her for days until she was well was dangerous. If the Starks or other men came onto the farm, how would she and Missouri Ann stand up to them? If they tried to stop the slave catchers from grabbing Sukey, Eliza and Missouri Ann might be hurt. And there were the children to think of. What if someone inquired about a colored woman? Would Davy and Luzena know enough to deny she was on the Spooner farm? They could be harmed, too. Eliza was conflicted. She'd agreed with Ettie that she wished there were something she could do for the Union, but did she have the right to risk the safety of others in the doing of it?

Remembering Ettie, she asked, "What about Mrs. Espy? She has older boys on the farm. Would she not be better at hiding the woman?"

John Hamlin smiled. "Last time she hid an escaped slave, the Starks almost caught him. I expect the man didn't get but five minutes head start, and the Starks would have found him at that, except the littlest Espy boy stepped on an iron spike and howled like the devil that he was going to get the lockjaw if somebody didn't help him."

"Did they get out the spike?" Missouri Ann asked.

"Turned out it was only a scrape, nothing to worry about. A boy of seven or thereabouts tricked them. The Starks were mad enough to chew nails. But that gave the slave enough time to get away. I reckon the Starks will go to the Espy place even before mine," John said. He turned to Eliza. "I wouldn't ask it, but there's a woman's life at stake."

And a woman who'd done nothing more than try to save the life of her son, Eliza thought. She and Missouri Ann would have done the same thing. In fact, Missouri Ann had already risked her own safety in getting Nance away from the Starks. But could she put the children in danger? Eliza wondered. She and Missouri Ann were grown women who knew the risks, but it wasn't fair to the children, especially Luzena, who did not fully understand about the war. Eliza pondered that, wishing Will could have given her advice, but she was on her own, and she must decide now. What would Will have told her to do? And then she knew. He would have advised her to do what was right. That was what he had said when he joined the army, that he did not care to go off and fight a war, but it was the right thing. He had died doing that right thing. Could she expect less of herself? It was not enough for men to do good, but women must, too. Eliza turned back to John. "Of course we shall take her in, Mr. Hamlin. And welcome her. It's what Will would have done. When will you bring her?"

"We have brought her already. She's in the wagon." He grinned as if he had known all along that Eliza would accept the slave.

Eliza turned to the wagon, which was filled with tree trunks. She had assumed John was taking them to the sawmill. "Where?"

"Under the timber."

"Why the poor thing!" Missouri Ann cried. "You likely crushed her."

"And if you didn't, she's bound to be uncomfortable," Eliza said. "We must take her inside at once."

While Eliza and Missouri Ann hurried to the house to prepare for the sick woman, Print drove the wagon close to the door. Then he and John removed the tree trunks that covered Sukey and lifted her out of her hiding place. They set her on her feet, but Sukey was so weak that she fell, and the men had to carry her inside the house. Eliza motioned for them to lay Sukey on the bed. The sick woman watched Eliza turn down the quilt, the Sunshine and Rain quilt that Eliza had put back on her bed after she learned of Will's death. Sukey was small, with small hands and feet, and she was as thin as a hoe handle. Her black eyes were quick, and they never left Eliza's face. When Eliza turned, she caught the slave's glance and read fear in it. Poor woman. She had suffered much and come far, and still she feared she would be caught and put to death. Maybe she wondered if Eliza would turn her in.

"You can trust me, Sukey. I am Mrs. Spooner, and this is Mrs. Stark, and we will care for you until you are well." Eliza thought a moment, then announced, "I would change her name. We would not want the children to let slip 'Sukey.' Do you understand?" she asked the slave. When Sukey nodded, Eliza announced, "Clara. Will you be Clara?"

Sukey nodded again and muttered, "Clara."

"Can you trust the children not to talk?" John asked.

"I will explain to them that it is a matter of life and death to keep silent about . . . Clara." Eliza smiled and glanced at the black woman when she said the name.

"Your daughter is young," John said, looking at Luzena, who had crept into the house. "Can you keep a secret, girl?"

"Yes, sir."

"You have kept other secrets?"

Luzena nodded.

"What secrets?"

Luzena raised her chin. "I won't tell you, sir. They're secrets."

John laughed. Then he spied Nance, who was hanging on to Luzena's skirt. "What about that one? She's too young to understand about secrets."

"Oh, that's all right," Missouri Ann told him. "She don't talk yet."

John said he and Print must leave, for they didn't want to alert anyone that they had stopped for more than a short visit at the Spooner farm. Sukey—Clara, he corrected himself—would be all right in the house as long as no one came looking for her, but they must find a hiding place for her just the same.

Missouri Ann suggested the soddy, where she and Nance slept, or the root cellar, but John told her anyone hunting the woman would look in those places.

Eliza said Clara might roll beneath the bed or under the straw in the barn, but John said men would check there, too. Then Luzena spoke up. "There's a hidey-hole in the haystack next to the

120

barn. I use it when I hide from Davy"—she glanced at her mother—"and Mama. Clara could go there."

Eliza nodded. "There's also a small hole under the floorboards where Will hid our valuables, but it's no bigger than a coffin."

"We've hidden contraband in smaller spaces, and it's better than no hiding place at all," John said. Then he cautioned, "You must not worry too much. The chances are good that no one will come here, but it is best to be prepared."

"Best for all of us," Eliza told him.

"Yes, it could go hard on you if the Starks or others found you had hidden her. I will come around when I can to check on Clara and inform you of the plans for her removal, but my visits might cause suspicion, so I must be judicious. Print has agreed to come in my place." He turned to Missouri Ann and said, "Please forgive my presumption, Mrs. Stark, but I think it might be got about that these are courting visits. That way, there will be no cause for comment."

"Except from those who might find the courting of a young widow offensive," Eliza told him. "But better we be gossiped about for lack of propriety than for hiding an escaped slave."

"I don't mind if Mr. Ritter don't," Missouri Ann said.

"Why, no, ma'am," he replied.

"That is good of you," Eliza said, then turned

away to hide her smile. John Hamlin seemed to be the only one in the room who didn't know that Print had already begun to court Missouri Ann.

From the doorway, Eliza and Missouri Ann watched as Print mounted his horse and John climbed into his wagon and both started down the lane to the road. Then the two women turned to Clara, who was lying on the bed, her eyes darting about. She was still afraid, Eliza knew, would be afraid until she reached Colorado, afraid until the terrible war was over. She might live in fear the rest of her life.

Davy came into the house with a pail of milk, and Clara gasped when she saw the boy.

"My son. He won't harm you," Eliza said. Then she explained to Davy why Clara was there.

Davy grinned. "This is as exciting as fighting Rebs. Any slave catchers come here, I'll shoot them."

Eliza said she hoped it wouldn't come to that. Clara would be there only a few days. Their job was to tend her and keep her safe. If any men came onto their land, Eliza and Missouri Ann would hide Clara in the haystack near the barn or in the hole in the floor. Eliza accepted the pail of milk from Davy and set it on the table. Then she took a dipperful and offered it to Clara, who drank it so quickly that Eliza wondered if the woman were starving. She found that a little of the chicken stew was left in the kettle and dished it into a bowl, handing it to Clara with a spoon.

Clara ignored the spoon and drank the stew, drank it so quickly that a little spilled on her dress. When she was finished, she examined the spoon, turning it over, then licked the dish. As she handed both back to Eliza, she said, "I never ate with no spoon before. Or a dish, neither."

Missouri Ann frowned. "How'd you eat, then?"

"My hands or clamshells in a trough in the yard, out back of the big house."

"Oh, how awful," Eliza said. "From now on, you will sit at the table with us and eat the way we do. We will have supper soon. I imagine you are still hungry."

Clara nodded, her eyes on the basket of eggs Luzena had brought into the house and the slab of salt pork Davy had fetched from the smokehouse.

"First, we'll see to your wounds," Eliza said. She sent Davy out to feed the animals, then she helped Clara remove her dress, which was filthy.

Eliza took out a shift for Clara to wear, while Missouri Ann volunteered to wash and mend the tattered garment. "There ain't much left to it, is there?" Missouri Ann observed, holding up the dress. Then she asked, "Where's your shoes?"

Clara shook her head. "Never had shoes."

Eliza thought it odd the colored woman did not cover herself when her dress was removed—she wore no undergarments—but only looked straight ahead dumbly, as if pretending she wasn't there. Modesty might be an extravagance for a slave, Eliza thought then, wondering what indignities the woman had suffered. Perhaps she was used to white people staring at her—white men. Eliza had heard that slaves were stripped naked on the auction block, so that buyers could examine them for imperfections. She was revolted by the idea that men had stared at the pretty slave as she stood there unclothed, perhaps touching her and making crude remarks. Clara would suffer no indignities in that house.

Eliza filled a pan with water, for Clara was as dirty as her dress. Then using soap and a soft cloth, she bathed the woman's face. When she was finished, she handed the cloth to Clara, who ran the wet rag over her thin body. "Never felt of soap on myself," Clara said. Eliza took back the cloth and told Clara to turn so that she could wash her back. When the slave did so, Eliza gasped. Clara's back was crisscrossed with ugly welts. Some were scabbed over, but others were angry with infection.

"Oh, Ma, what happened to her back?" Luzena burst out.

"She was whipped," Eliza replied. "You see, Luzena, that is one reason your father died fighting to end slavery. No person, especially a woman, deserves to be treated like this." She felt proud of Will.

"She must have been awful bad to get whipped that way," Luzena said.

"No, she didn't do anything."

"You got any liniment?" Missouri Ann asked. "That's what Mother Stark puts on the dogs when they get whipped. Heals them right up. She uses brandy and turpentine and camphor gum. Maybe beef gall if you got it." She paused. "But even a Stark wouldn't beat a dog that way."

"I use honey and beeswax and turpentine," Eliza said, going to the cupboard and taking down the ingredients, which she combined in a bowl. She spread the mixture on Clara's back, and though the slave winced, she didn't utter a word. "You're a brave woman, Clara," Eliza said after she was finished dressing the wounds and bandaging them with strips of cloth. She slipped the shift over Clara's head.

While Eliza cared for Clara, Luzena fried the salt pork and the eggs, and placed the food on a platter, which she set on the table along with cornbread and a pitcher of milk.

"It isn't much, but it's the best we can offer in these hard times," Eliza explained.

"I hardly never got a taste of egg before," Clara said. She held back, while the others seated themselves.

Eliza started to bow her head, but when she saw that Clara was still sitting on the bed, waiting, she said, "Come along. You will eat with us, Clara. Sit beside Nance." She pointed to the little girl. After Clara joined them, Eliza bowed her head again. Until Will's death, Eliza had prayed that he would come home unharmed. Now she asked help in keeping Clara safe. Perhaps God would do a better job this time.

Eliza served Clara first—after all, she was a guest—then remembering the woman had said that on the plantation, she'd eaten from a trough using a clamshell for a utensil, Eliza gave her a spoon, thinking a fork might confuse the girl. Clara did not wait until the others were served, but picked up the plate and spooned the food into her mouth, finishing before Eliza had begun to eat. Then Clara tore off a chunk of cornbread, stuffing it into her mouth.

"She eats too fast," Luzena observed.

Eliza thought to reprimand her daughter for her rudeness, but instead, she explained, "If there is not enough food and you fear someone else will take it all, you would eat quickly, too."

After she finished eating, Clara demanded, "Where's your man?"

"He was killed fighting for the Union," Eliza answered.

"And yourn?" she asked Missouri Ann.

"Dead. He was a soldier, too."

"Ain't no man here?"

"I am," Davy spoke up.

"You only a boy."

Davy would be good protection, Eliza explained. He could shoot a gun as well as his father, and so could she and Missouri Ann.

"I never saw no lady with a gun." Clara thought that over. "Maybe you ain't ladies. You're womens."

"In the North," Eliza told her, "we are both."

Through the night, Eliza heard Clara moan and thrash about, once calling out, "No, mist'ess." Missouri Ann was sleeping in the loft that night with the children, so Eliza rose from the pallet beside the bed, to attend the slave. It was a wonder that the poor thing could sleep at all with her pain and suffering. In the morning, Clara was almost out of her mind with fever. She muttered, "Joe," over and over in her sleep, until Eliza told Missouri Ann that Joe must have been Clara's son. During the day, Eliza, Missouri Ann, and Luzena took turns sponging the woman's face and arms with cool water. Clara slept only fitfully. Once she awoke and sat upright and blurted out, "Lord Jesus going send you to hell." Then toward evening, she fell into a deep sleep. At first, Eliza was thankful, hoping that meant Clara's fever had broken, but at dinnertime, when she tried to awaken Clara, Eliza wondered if the woman was in a coma. If that were so, there was nothing Eliza could do about it.

• • •

Although neither Eliza or Missouri Ann wanted to leave the house the next morning, work had to be done. They had skipped an entire day of hoeing because of the quilting bee and had spent the next day hovering over Clara. They could not sacrifice a third day. So the two left Clara in Luzena's care and went to the near field, finding chores that would take them to the barn or close to the house to check on the sick woman. Luzena stayed inside with Clara, latching the door each time someone left and demanding to know the identity of anyone who wanted to come inside.

Once when Eliza returned to the house, she found Luzena pretending she was on a wagon train going to the gold fields. It had been her favorite game when she was small, and now she'd set up the wagon train for Nance, stretching a quilt over two chairs facing away from each other, putting a third chair at one end for a wagon seat. Then she'd arranged the two bears that Eliza had made for Luzena when she was a baby and stuffed with chicken feathers, in front of the chairs as oxen. They did look a little more like oxen than bears, Eliza decided. With her doll, Miss Cat, on one side, Nance on the other, Luzena sat on one of the chairs with a string tied to a stick for a whip and called to the oxen to hurry along. "I'm taking Clara to Colorado where she'll be safe, but the oxen move right poorly today, Mama," Luzena said, as she let Eliza into the room, then secured the door.

"So do I," Eliza replied. "It's the heat."

"I should have bought me mules for the trip."

Laughing at the silly game, Eliza tiptoed across the room and examined Clara. The woman still was in a deep sleep.

"Is she going to get better?" Luzena asked.

"Yes, I believe she will. The greater danger is someone trying to steal her away. It's best you keep the curtain drawn across the window."

What if someone came while Eliza was in the fields? Luzena asked.

"If you are outside, you must ring the dinner bell to summon us. If you are inside, then keep the door bolted. Don't open it to anyone but Missouri Ann, Davy, or me."

"I wish Papa was here. He'd shoot anybody who tried to take Clara."

Eliza nodded her agreement. She had never felt so keenly the loss of her husband. Will would have protected them, would have stood up to anyone who tried to take Clara. Despite her brave talk of the day before, Eliza was uneasy, afraid of what might happen with only two women and two children and a baby to protect the hunted slave. "Oh, Will," she whispered to herself. "It is so hard without you." She turned toward the door so that Luzena would not see how distraught she was.

Outside, Eliza walked to the bend in the lane, looking up and down the road to see if there was dust from a wagon or a horse, but the air was still, and she thought Clara would indeed be safe. It would be only a day or two before the woman was well enough to continue her journey.

But Clara did not heal quickly. "She is dangerous ill," Eliza told Print Ritter when he called that evening. The family had heard him ride up and had stared at each other before Davy jumped up and took down the shotgun and Eliza went to the window and peered out from the edge of the curtain.

"Hello the house," Print called. "It's the blacksmith come for a visit."

Eliza sighed with relief, while Missouri Ann smoothed her hair and took off her apron. Davy looked disappointed as he drew out the board from brackets bolted to either side of the door frame. The board kept anyone from forcing the door. As Print entered the room, Clara, who had been sleeping, suddenly sat up and drew against the wall, the quilt twisted in her hands.

"It's all right, dear," Eliza said. "It's only Mr. Ritter. You know him. He brought you here."

Clara seemed confused, and Eliza wondered if the slave remembered arriving at the Spooner house. Perhaps with her delirium, she didn't even remember Eliza. "You are safe," Eliza said, putting her arm around Clara, who winced, and Eliza remembered the terrible wounds. She turned to Print and said, "Mr. Ritter, Clara has had a bad time of it. It would be dangerous for her to leave just yet."

Print nodded. "There's danger out there, too. It's rumored in town that she's in the vicinity, and slave catchers have been looking for her from Genesis to Revelations. I've overheard them at the smithy. We'll have to wait and hope they give up."

"The others might give up but not the Starks, Mr. Ritter," Missouri Ann said. "They'll want that reward. These are squirrel-food times for them."

"Pity they don't go to work then," Print said.

"Oh, Starks don't work. They only steal."

"How come you married one then?" Davy spoke up.

Eliza sought to hush him, but Missouri Ann replied, "My husband was different. He was a good man." She looked at Nance when she said that, and Eliza thought what a difficult thing it would be to raise a little girl who'd know her family was mean and spiteful. Missouri Ann was right to praise Hugh.

"Where will you take Clara next?"

"It's best you don't know. The less you know, the safer she is. And you, too."

"Would you have a bite of supper?" Eliza asked Print. "We are about to sit to it." She had killed a chicken and boiled it, thinking the broth would strengthen Clara. And there was corn-bread, dandelion greens, and sauce that Luzena had made from dried apples, saying if she were sick, that was what she would like to eat.

"I wouldn't want to rob you," Print said.

"Sit, Mr. Ritter. We would welcome the presence of a man in this dangerous time." She pointed to Will's place at the table, which had been empty since he went away to war. Then she and Missouri Ann helped Clara to the chair at the other end, while the rest of them sat down on benches on either side. Clara sagged in the chair and could barely pick up her spoon, and Eliza said, "You see how weak she is, Mr. Ritter. The fever has passed, but it will be another day or two before she can take more than a few steps." She lowered her voice, although Clara didn't seem to be paying attention. "Her back was whipped to shreds. It is a miracle she survived. How could anyone do such a thing to another human being?"

"You understand now why we care so much about helping people like her escape," Print replied.

"And I know what my husband fought and died for."

Clara slept late into the morning two days later and had not yet awakened when Eliza and Missouri Ann left the house. When they returned at noon, the slave sat on the bed, her fever gone, one of the bed quilts in her hand, stitching.

"She found a place where the quilt was torn and asked for a needle," Luzena said. "I'd sew, too, but the oxen aren't behaving today." The girl had set up the wagon train again for Nance.

Clara held up the quilt for Eliza's inspection. She had mended not only the torn spot but other places where the stitching had come loose.

"Such tiny stitches. I myself could not match them."

"I work in the big house, stitched all mist'ess' clothes. Then she sent me to the fields." She frowned and was silent.

"Did you make quilts, too?"

"I did. Made my own squares. I help you with your top, you want me to."

Eliza clapped her hands. "I wish I could stay and stitch with you."

"Well, why don't you?" Missouri Ann said. Eliza could join her later in the field.

"You wouldn't mind? I won't stay more than a few minutes. My hands itch to piece."

"Do you good," Missouri Ann told her.

After Missouri Ann was gone, Eliza bolted the door, then took out her piecing. "Why were you sent to the fields?" she asked, by way of making conversation.

"My boy looked just like the master," Clara replied. "Mist'ess don't want me around."

133

Eliza was ashamed of herself. She should have remembered that the mistress's husband had fathered Clara's child. "I ask you to forgive me," she said, and bent over her sewing.

"Ain't nothing to forgive." Clara paused. "I try to forgive the mist'ess for taking away my Joe and the master that sold my husband, but I can't."

"You had a husband? And he was sold?" Eliza couldn't help blurting out.

"Me and him jumped the broomstick when I was 'bout fourteen. He stood up to the master when he come to the cabin, and the master don't like that. So he sells Billy. I won't never see him again. He's dead to me, just like your husband."

The mention of Will made Eliza look up. "My husband truly is dead, but couldn't you find your Billy, maybe after this war is done with?"

"How?" Clara asked.

"You could go back."

Clara shook her head. "Not till Resurrection Day. They'd kill me."

"Then you are a widow as much as I and Mrs. Stark. All three of us have lost half of who we are," Eliza told her. She folded the sewing and stood up, saying it was time for Clara to rest. As she left, she warned Luzena to bolt the door.

"We'll never get to Colorado with the door closed," Luzena told Nance as they sat in the make-believe covered wagon.

When Eliza reached the field, Missouri Ann observed, "Clara quilts as good as you."

"Better, except maybe for Will's Stars and Stripes." Eliza was thinking of the Christmas quilt, wondering again what had become of it. Then she heard the dinner bell and knew there was trouble.

CHAPTER SIX

April 3, 1865

Davy was the first to hear the mules. He had been forking fresh straw into the horse's stall when he heard the men ride up, and he rushed outside. When he saw Dad Stark and three of his sons mounted on mules, he ran to the dinner bell, mounted on a post, and pulled the rope back and forth, until one of the Stark boys came up beside him, pushed him aside, and stilled the bell.

Off in the field, Eliza and Missouri Ann heard the clanging. "Run," Eliza called, and the two dropped their hoes and bolted for the house.

The Starks sat on their mules, taking their time, smirking at the fear on Davy's face and the anguish of the two women who came running into the barnyard, gasping for breath. Missouri Ann lifted her apron and ran it across her wet face.

With a contemptuous glare, Dad Stark looked Missouri Ann up and down and said, "So they turned you into a field hand, did they, girlie?"

She didn't answer. Instead, she said, "You're

drunk as a fiddler, Dad Stark. You come here to make trouble for me? Get on home."

"Blamed if we will," said Amos, one of the sons.

"This is my property. You are not welcome here, Mr. Stark," Eliza told him. "You and your boys are trespassing. You'd best be on your way." Her hands were damp, and she rubbed them on her skirt.

Dad Stark shifted on his mule and spat tobacco juice at Eliza's feet. "Don't be telling me what to do, missus. You and Missouri Ann and that pup there ain't big enough to take us on. We'll leave when we get what we come for."

"Missouri Ann is not going with you. The reverend told you to keep away from her. You know that," Eliza said. She hoped the Starks would believe she assumed their reason for coming to the Spooner farm was to fetch Missouri Ann. She would pretend she knew nothing about a runaway slave, of course.

"Oh, we didn't come for her. She's worthless. Edison don't want her anyway. We come for the slave girl."

"I believe Mr. Lincoln abolished slavery, although that is beside the point. We do not believe in human bondage. There are no slaves on this farm. Surely you are aware of that, Mr. Stark." Despite her words, Eliza almost shook with fear.

"I don't care about that damn-fool Lincoln. Slavery's still legal south of here. And murder ain't. She's a killer. We ain't leaving without the colored girl."

"I don't know what you're talking about. We haven't seen a colored girl."

Dad Stark gave a bark of a laugh, showing his stained teeth, and spat a wad of tobacco onto the ground, while Taft and Amos Stark dismounted and started for the barn.

"Hey, you can't go in there," Davy said. He took a step toward them, the hay fork in his hand.

Taft swatted it away. "Step aside, boy," he said. "We got business here." He ripped the implement from Davy's hand, saying it might come in handy.

Davy glanced at Eliza, who dropped her eyes to let him know not to confront the men, and he and the two women watched as the brothers disappeared into the barn. After a time, they came out shaking their heads. "She ain't hid there, Pa," Amos said.

"Check that haystack. Blamed abolitionists always hide slaves in haystacks."

As Amos jabbed the fork into the hay, Eliza held her breath, hoping Luzena had not had time to secrete Clara there. The sharp prongs went in and out, but they hit nothing solid, and Eliza decided that Luzena must have hidden Clara under the floorboards in the house.

Dad Stark and his third son, Ben, dismounted. "Where's the woman?" Dad Stark demanded, coming so close to Eliza that the animal scent of him repulsed her.

"I've told you that there is no slave here. Why would you think we are hiding anyone?" she asked.

"We followed Print Ritter when he come to your house last night. He's got no other business here."

Eliza glanced at Missouri Ann, who seemed to cower now under the man's gaze, her bravery gone. It was not Eliza's place to say why Print had visited, and she thought her friend might be frightened to tell her former father-in-law that she was being courted.

Missouri Ann fidgeted and wouldn't look Dad Stark in the eye. Finally she said in a low voice, "Ain't your business if he comes courting."

"Courting!" Dad Stark burst out. "Girl, you ain't been a widow six months. You dishonor my son. You ain't worthy of the name Stark." Dad ran his hand through his hair and scratched his head. "It ain't enough to knock you down. I ought to take a whip to you. You think you moved in with the quality and are living white-bread times. Why, you're no better than a whore."

"Mr. Stark!" Eliza said. "I will have no such language on my farm."

"What are you going to do about it? I got three

grown men with me, and you're nothing but a couple of women and a boy."

Eliza put her hand out to stop Davy from taking a step forward, thinking how unjust the times were. Will was dead, but these worthless men were alive and well.

"You just tell me what you done with that slave girl, and you can throw Missouri Ann and her worthless whelp to the hogs, for all I care," Dad Stark continued.

"And you can go to hell for all I care," Missouri Ann told him.

"You ain't got the right to talk to me that way!" Dad Stark flung back his hand and slapped Missouri Ann across the face. "You watch your tongue, or I'll toss you over my mule and take you back to marry Edison. Lord knows why that boy fancies you, or Hugh, neither. I never understood why he'd marry a puny thing like you that ain't woman enough for a Stark, when he could have got any woman in Wabaunsee County. You tricked him into it, getting yourself in the family way. Maybe that girl of yours, that Nance, ain't Hugh's at all. Starks spawn boys."

"How can you say it!" Missouri Ann cried.

Missouri Ann's face was dark where Dad Stark had slapped her, and Eliza knew there would be an ugly bruise. She was afraid the man might live up to his threat to snatch up Missouri Ann, so she stepped forward. "We have nothing to hide.

You have my permission to search the farm," she said, knowing the men would do that whether she agreed to it or not. "And when you are finished, you are to leave."

"Don't need your permission," Dad Stark replied. He threw out his hand to indicate to his sons that they were to look about the farm. Amos went to the soddy, where Eliza could hear him throwing things about. In a moment, he came outside, holding a quilt, saying maybe their mother would like it.

Eliza started to protest. Missouri Ann had made the quilt top just after Christmas, had pieced a giant star for the center and smaller stars to surround it. The two women had quilted the coverlet on snowy winter evenings. "No—" Eliza said, but Missouri Ann touched her arm.

"It's all right," she said softly. "It's for Mother Stark."

Dad Stark studied her a moment, then smirked. "Or maybe for one of the mules. Might make a good saddle blanket."

Missouri Ann refused to rise to the bait. "Maybe."

Eliza stared at the old man, but out of the corner of her eye, she watched the Stark boys as they moved from the soddy to the smokehouse to the storm cellar. "Not in here, neither," Ben said, coming up the storm cellar steps carrying a crock of dried peaches. "Want some of these, Pa?" he asked, reaching into the crock and removing a handful of fruit, dropping some onto the ground. Eliza pursed her lips. She had traded for a bushel of peaches the summer before, had dried them herself, and was saving them for something special, maybe a peach pie on Independence Day. But she would not anger the Starks by ordering Ben to return the crock to the cellar.

"Never liked a peach," Dad said, and Ben upended the crock, dropping the peaches in the dirt.

The Stark boys finished searching the farm. "I guess she ain't here," Dad Stark said, and then toying with Eliza and Missouri Ann, he added, "Oh, I forgot. We ain't looked in the house yet. You think maybe somebody hid her in there?" He grinned at Eliza, as if he had told a joke.

Eliza stared straight ahead, hoping her face did not betray her fear. She said nothing, as Ben and Taft went to the house and tried the door. It was latched. Taft attempted to shove it, but the door held firm. "It's bolted from inside, Pa," Taft said.

"Well, I guess I know that, don't I?" Dad Stark said. "You think I don't got eyes?" He turned to Eliza. "You tell whoever's in there to open it up."

Eliza did not answer, only straightened her back and stared at the man.

"Unbolt the house," Dad Stark yelled.

The curtain in the window moved, but there was no reply. Then the shutter inside the house closed, and Eliza knew Luzena had fastened it. Although Luzena must be frightened, she had acted with steadfastness. Eliza was proud of her. Will would have been proud of her. The Starks could no more break into the house through the window than they could shove open the door. Luzena would keep the place closed up until the Starks gave up or someone came along the road to help. Maybe Print or even John Hamlin would have a notion something was wrong.

"Can't get in, Pa," Ben said.

Dad Stark scowled at his son and told him he had a way of saying stupid things. He demanded to know who was inside, but Eliza refused to answer.

Then Taft spoke up and said that Eliza had a chunk of a girl and that she must be inside the house.

"We ain't letting no girl stop us." Dad Stark turned to Eliza. "You tell her to open the door or we'll burn the place down."

"Can't burn it down, Pa," Ben told him. "It'd take two days for that hard wood to catch fire."

Dad Stark ran a dirty finger over his teeth. Then suddenly, he reached over and grabbed Eliza by the hair. "Girl in there, you open that door or your ma'll get hurt," he yelled.

"He won't do anything, Luzena," Eliza called.

"You just watch out that window and see if I won't." Dad Stark tightened his grasp on Eliza's hair with one hand, pulling her up until she was standing on her toes. With his other hand, he twisted Eliza's arm behind her back. She struggled and kicked, but her tormentor only laughed. Davy lunged forward and raised his hand to Dad Stark, but Amos grabbed him, while Taft held on to Missouri Ann. Davy bit Amos's arm, and the man punched the boy in the stomach, making him double over. "You're a coward, Amos, hitting a boy," Missouri Ann cried, but Amos only grinned and saluted her with his free hand like a soldier.

Eliza saw the shutter open a crack and knew that Luzena was watching, had seen the attacks on her mother and brother. "Stay inside. They're bluffing," she called.

"Oh, we are, are we?" Dad Stark slapped Eliza hard, back and forth, then dropped her to the ground. "You want worse for her, girl? We'll do your brother next," he called. "All you got to do is open the door, and we'll leave be." When the door remained closed, Dad Stark dismounted, kicked at Eliza, who was lying on the ground, and started for Davy. "I reckon he don't need his left arm," he yelled. "You ever see anybody get his arm tore off?"

Davy's face went pale, and his legs were so limp that he would have fallen if Amos had not held on to him. Still, he called in a frightened voice, "Don't you believe them, Luzena." Eliza felt useless. How could she and Missouri Ann and Davy stand off four men? If only Will were there, but he would never be there. The unfairness of it all! Eliza thought.

The threats were enough to crumble the girl's resolve, and Eliza heard the bolt being drawn, then saw the door open. The Starks forgot about Eliza and Davy and rushed forward. Missouri Ann helped Eliza and Davy to their feet, and the three followed the Starks into the house.

"I couldn't let them hurt you or Davy that way, Mama," Luzena cried, tears running down her face. "I know you said to protect Nance with my life, but I couldn't do it if they were going to hurt Davy. Don't let them take her."

"We don't care a rotten apple for the baby. We come for the black girl. Where's she hid?" Dad Stark demanded.

Luzena looked at him blankly. "What's he talking about?" she asked her mother. Dad Stark pinched Luzena's arm and the girl winced. "I don't know anything," she said.

"You got a colored girl hid around here somewheres."

"I've never seen a colored girl in my life. It's just me and Nance. We're playing covered wagon. We're going to the gold fields." Luzena sat down on one of the quilt-covered chairs and picked up her doll, muttering, "Aren't we, Miss Cat? We're going to get rich, aren't we?"

"You'd be going to hell if you hadn't opened that door," Dad Stark said. "And maybe you will yet, if we don't find that girl." He tore the bed apart while two of his boys climbed the ladder to the loft. Eliza held her twisted arm as she stared upstairs, listening to the Starks turn over the beds and throw the dresser drawers onto the floor. Then they clumped down the ladder, shaking their heads. One of the boys looked into the fireplace, while another went around the room, searching for loose logs that might have allowed someone to escape. Eliza refused to glance at the floorboards, afraid she might give away the hiding place.

At last, Ben said, "I think maybe she ain't here, Pa."

"You hush your mouth. I'll do the thinking." Dad Stark looked around at the walls, then up at the roof, and finally at the floor. He stared at the floor for a long time, and then he kicked at a board that was loose. It was a full inch higher than the others. "What we got here?" he asked.

As Eliza closed her eyes and prayed, Dad Stark's sons gathered around him. Eliza opened her eyes and exchanged a glance with Missouri Ann. Then she reached for the poker, which was resting near the fireplace. There was no way she could stop the men from taking Clara, but at least one of the Starks would go away wounded. Missouri Ann, taking her cue from Eliza, picked up a skillet. Davy raised his eyes to the shotgun over the fireplace, but Eliza shook her head. He wouldn't have time to load it, and even if he did, one of the Starks would grab it from Davy, and the boy might get shot.

Only Luzena seemed to ignore what was going on, as she slapped the string-reins over the backs of the stuffed animals that acted as oxen and urged them on to Colorado. Eliza thought to quiet her, but Luzena had suffered a terrible shock what with the men threatening her mother and brother, and she seemed to have slipped into another world. Eliza wondered if her daughter's mind had been affected.

Dad Stark kicked at the board again, but it held, so he squatted beside it and grasped it with his hands, pulling it up. "Why, lookit here. What we got is a hidey-hole beneath." He grinned at Missouri Ann. "What do you think of that?" When Missouri Ann refused to answer, he made a fist and said, "You can't get too big not to speak to me." He started to rise, but Amos told him that another board was loose, and Dad Stark grasped it and yanked it out, too. "This whole floor's just one big hole," he said.

The men grabbed at the floorboards, and in a moment, they revealed a hole the size of a shallow grave. Ben, the smallest of the Starks, climbed into it, then lifted his head and laughed as he held up his arm. In his hand was a gallon jug of whiskey. Eliza almost smiled. Will had found a hiding place for his liquor. He'd had a fondness for drink sometimes.

"What else you got in there?" Amos asked, grabbing the bottle. "Maybe there's more of this."

Ben rummaged around in the hole then emerged empty-handed. "No more whiskey, and no more nothing else, neither."

"What about the girl? Ain't she in there?" Dad Stark demanded.

Ben shook his head.

"Aw, let me see." Dad Stark pushed his son aside and climbed into the hole himself. A moment later, he pushed himself up onto the floor, his hands covered with dirt, as if he'd been scratching around in the earth. "She ain't here." He turned to Eliza. "Where's she at?" He had lost some of his bluster.

"I told you, she isn't here," Eliza said, trying not to show her surprise. She'd been sure that Luzena had hidden Clara under the floorboards. Perhaps the slave had left on her own, before the Starks arrived, when Eliza was in the field with Missouri Ann. That was the only explanation she could think of. But now that Clara was gone, Eliza felt more confident. "You've called me a liar and other foul epithets, and you have all but destroyed my home, Mr. Stark. You profane my farm. And you've frightened my children. It is a mean practice, this hunting of a free colored woman."

"Then how come your girl there wouldn't let us in the house if she wasn't hiding the slave?" Dad Stark asked. "Tell me that."

"You scared her almost to death, four bullies riding into the barnyard and threatening her mother and brother. Surely you understand why she secured herself and the baby. She was afraid you would harm Nance. You scared her out of her wits. You can see it for yourself."

As if to prove the point, Luzena began to hum "O, Susannah!" under her breath as she urged the play oxen to hurry west. Her singing grew louder until it was almost a screech. Then she stopped and said, "We're going to find a gold mine, Mama." She began singing off key again.

"I hope her mind is not permanently damaged," Eliza added.

"Women's ain't got much of a mind to speak of," Dad Stark replied, glaring at Luzena as if the look would make the girl be quiet. But Luzena kept on, louder now.

Eliza straightened up and put her hands on her hips. "I will not put up with such nonsense. Get out of here, Mr. Stark. Get out, all of you, right now, or I shall notify the sheriff of your mischief. You are cowards and kidnappers."

The Stark boys turned to their father, who slowly got to his feet. "You got no right to call us that."

"What else would you call four men who break

into a house in an attempt to steal away a slave girl?"

"She really going to go to the sheriff?" Taft asked.

Eliza was sorry for the threat and realized she needed to give the Starks a way out, some reassurance that it was better for them to leave than to stay. Not only could they overpower her, but their very presence threatened Clara. If Clara was hidden nearby, Eliza wanted the men off the farm. So she said, "I would not embarrass Missouri Ann by reporting her in-laws as law breakers. But if you set foot on this farm again, I shall tell everyone in Wabaunsee County of your outrageous conduct." She went to the doorway and pointed outside.

Dad Stark looked around the house once more, then nodded at his sons. "Might be she's at the Espy place. That old woman would hide a yellow dog if she knew we was after it."

Dad Stark clomped out of the house, followed by Taft and Amos. Ben was last, and he touched the brim of his hat at Missouri Ann.

"Tell Mother Stark I said howdy," Missouri Ann told him. "Tell her come for a visit."

Ben didn't reply, and Eliza wasn't sure he had heard Missouri Ann.

While Luzena continued to drive her team, Eliza, Davy, and Missouri Ann went outside to watch the Starks mount up and ride off. Davy followed them to the end of the lane to make sure the men were gone for good. He asked Eliza if he should warn Ettie Espy.

"Not yet. Let's find out if Clara is headed that way first." Eliza turned to her daughter, who had stopped singing as soon as the Starks were gone, and asked, "Where is she, Luzena? What have you done with Clara?"

Luzena stood, then went to the door and closed and bolted it. Then for good measure, she latched the window. "It's safe, Clara," she whispered. She went back to the covered wagon. "Come on out. They're gone."

Slowly, the quilt that was spread over the two chairs to form the covered wagon moved, and Clara crawled out. She looked exhausted, and she shook as she tried to stand. "They gone away?" she asked.

Missouri Ann's mouth dropped open in surprise, while Eliza began to laugh. "Why, you hid her in plain sight," Eliza said, grasping the slave and helping her to the bed. "I know every inch of this house, and even I wouldn't have suspected you were there."

Luzena blushed at the praise. "When I heard those men, I tried to put her in the hole, but I couldn't get the board out. It was too heavy. This was the only place I could think of. I thought if I acted crazy, they might not come too close." She looked inquiringly at her mother and Missouri Ann.

"You did good, real good," Missouri Ann said.

Eliza nodded her agreement. "To think a twelve-year-old girl fooled four grown men."

"But not very smart ones," Missouri Ann muttered.

"Shrewd, though," Eliza said. She asked Missouri Ann if the Starks would come back.

"I don't know," Missouri Ann told her. "They're tricky, but they wouldn't want to be shamed again. I couldn't say. I never could figure out how a Stark thought." She paused and added, "That is, if a Stark thinks at all. Best we find another place to hide Clara."

At nightfall, they heard hoofbeats in the lane, and Missouri Ann smoothed her hair and said it must be Print Ritter.

But something made Eliza wary. She peered out the window at the drizzle that was falling from the sky and saw a mule and knew it wasn't Print. He rode a horse. Then Eliza realized that the rider wore a bonnet. But she didn't know any woman who rode astride.

"Let me see," Missouri Ann said, peering into the darkness. "Why, it's Mother Stark."

Eliza was startled and started to shut the window. "What does she want? Did she come to spy for her husband?"

"She wouldn't do that," Missouri Ann assured

her, putting up her hand to keep the window open. She went to the door and opened it a crack, while Davy took down the shotgun. This time, Eliza didn't stop him. "Is that you, Mother Stark?" Missouri Ann called.

"It is, and I'm alone. But I got to hurry. Dad thinks I went for the borrow of a needle. If I don't get back soon, he might send the boys looking for me."

Dad Stark would be too drunk to go himself, Missouri Ann whispered to Eliza.

"Would you let me in the house?" the old woman asked. "This weather gets to my bones."

Missouri Ann turned to Eliza, telling her, "Mother Stark is as good as pie." Eliza wasn't so sure, and she sent Clara up to the loft to hide, before Missouri Ann opened the door wide and gestured for Mother Stark to get off her mule and come inside.

Mother Stark was a tall, big-boned woman, but she was gaunt, her face dark from the sun. She wore a ragged shawl, and her skirt was worn and patched. She was barefoot. Eliza, who had met her only once or twice, was drawn to the old woman, sure that she had been mistreated by her husband and maybe her sons. "Come in. We have a fire, and the remains of dinner. Would you have a bite?" She gestured to the table, realizing it held six plates. She grabbed them up, hoping Mother Stark had not had time to count them. The Stark men wouldn't have noticed the number of plates, but a woman would.

If she had, Mother Stark didn't comment. "I could use a pone, if you got any."

"Wheat bread," Eliza said.

"Wheat bread." Mother Stark sighed. "I ain't ate wheat bread in a long time."

"I can fry up some bacon," Eliza said, spreading butter on a piece of bread that she cut twice as thick as usual, but Mother Stark shook her head.

"Ain't time." As she crammed the bread into her mouth, Mother Stark glanced around and spotted Nance, who was hopping from one foot to another in excitement. "Baby Nance! You come to your old granny," she cried, opening her arms. "I love this child more'n I love side meat."

The little girl ran to her grandmother, and the old woman swooped her up in an embrace, telling Nance how much she had missed her. "I loved all my children when they was little like this, but I was gladdest when my baby-making days was over. I had twelve, my own self, and lost the best ones. Them boys that lived turned out just like their pa, the tobacco-chewing old scamp."

Eliza was about to ask if she didn't believe Hugh was better than the others, but she held her tongue. The Stark woman hadn't come to talk about her boys.

Mother Stark settled Nance on her lap, then leaned forward. "I won't ask where you got the colored girl hid. I don't want to know, because I don't want to lie to Dad if he finds out I been here and puts the leather to me."

Eliza put her hand over her mouth at the news that Dad Stark beat his wife, and with a leather strap or a whip! No wonder Missouri Ann felt protective of her mother-in-law. Eliza sat down on the bench beside the old woman and took her hand. "Such an awful thing," she said.

"Oh, I'm used to it. The boys make sure he don't do it too hard. Missouri Ann stood up for me once, and he took to her bad, until Edison made him stop. He sure would like you to come back, Missouri Ann, but don't you do it. I love my boys, but I know they got their ways. I was gladdest when you got away. I waited too long." Mother Stark combed Nance's fine hair with her fingers, and Eliza thought it was a shame the woman had never had daughters who'd lived. They would have been a comfort to her, as Missouri Ann apparently had been. The old woman must be lonely with her daughter-in-law gone.

The wind knocked a branch against the house, and Mother Stark looked up sharply. "I best be going back. I come to warn you, Missouri Ann. You, too, Mrs. Spooner. Dad and the boys are coming back at sunup. They know you got the girl hid somewheres, and they'll tear up the place to find her. Wherever you got her, you get her out of there." Mother Stark held Nance close. Then she stood up. "Oh, I almost forgot." She reached under her shawl and pulled out a cloth sack.

"My scrap bag!" Missouri Ann cried, snatching it.

"I knowed you prized it, and I kept it hid until such time as I could give it to you," Mother Stark said, pleasure in her voice at Missouri Ann's excitement. "I used a scrap or two myself, but most's there."

"Why, you good old thing," Missouri Ann said, and impulsively put her arms around the old woman.

"Now, now, don't carry on so," Mother Stark said, embarrassed, and pulled back. "I got to go now."

Eliza cut another slice of bread and spread butter on it, then handed it to Mother Stark. "We appreciate your warning, but tell me, why did you risk yourself by coming here?"

"Oh, it wouldn't go easy with Missouri Ann if Dad found out she'd tricked him. And she's as near like a daughter as I ever had." The old woman looked down at the floorboards as if embarrassed. "I never told nobody—Dad wouldn't like it—but I never held with slavery. Being a wife sometimes is as near being a slave as a body can get, and it ain't a good thing. I wouldn't like to see that poor colored girl dragged home and hanged from a tree. Now I

156

best get before Dad misses me." She reached out and touched Missouri Ann's hand, but except for Baby Nance, Mother Stark apparently was not a hugging woman, so she didn't embrace Missouri Ann. "You take a care, girl."

"I'll come for a visit and maybe bring you a spool of thread, if you don't mind," Missouri Ann said.

"Don't you do it. Don't you come back, not for me, not even for a visit." She glanced wistfully at Baby Nance and said, "I'd give a spool of thread for this one."

Missouri Ann squeezed the woman's hand, then she and Eliza walked outside with her, into the rain. The rain was good. It would hide the mule's tracks, Eliza thought.

Mother Stark flung her leg over the mule, just like a man, and said, "You take care of that precious baby. I never missed nobody so much in my life." She kicked the mule and rode off.

Eliza watched until Mother Stark disappeared in the darkness. Then she turned and rushed to the house. Clara couldn't hide in Luzena's covered wagon again. The Starks wouldn't be fooled a second time. Eliza would have to find a safer spot for her. But where? The men had already searched the places Clara could hide—the barn, the soddy—and they would surely search them again. Clara was too sick to run out into the fields in the rain. Besides, the men were likely to look there, too. Clara would have to go elsewhere. But where? Certainly not to John Hamlin's farm or to Ettie Espy's. The Starks would suspect both places. She went over the neighbors who might hide the woman, and then she knew. There was one place the Starks would never look. "Hitch up the buggy, Davy," Eliza said. "I'm taking Clara off the farm."

"Where?" Missouri Ann asked.

"To Mercy Eagles's place."

"But she ain't against slavery. She said so at the quilting. She said it in town, too," Missouri Ann protested.

"That makes her farm the ideal place to hide Clara."

CHAPTER SEVEN

April 3, 1865

With Clara wrapped in a quilt and huddled beside her, Eliza drove the buggy down the lane and out onto the main road. Eliza feared the Starks might be waiting for her at the turn, although Mother Stark had assured her the men would not come to the farm until dawn. She'd said they had finished Will's jug of whiskey before they reached home, and once there, they'd started on their own corn liquor. They'd fallen asleep and wouldn't wake for a while. When he wasn't being mean, Dad Stark was either drinking or sleeping, Missouri Ann had told Eliza. "He's got a gizzard for a heart," she said.

It wasn't just the Starks who made Eliza uneasy. If they weren't on the road, others might be. After all, John had warned the Starks weren't the only slave catchers who would be looking for Clara. And then there were always the tramps, the discharged soldiers and deserters, who would not hesitate to stop a woman driving a buggy late at night. She'd thought of bringing Luzena with her so that she could explain the child was sick and she was taking her to the doctor. But the doctor lived in the opposite direction. Besides, anyone stopping the buggy would see Clara curled up inside. Moreover, Luzena had already played a heroic part in keeping Clara safe. Eliza did not want to cause the girl further anguish.

The night was dark, with only a sliver of moon visible through the clouds. The hard rain kept falling, and the wind blew drops into the conveyance. Although she wished the skies would clear, Eliza knew that the rain offered protection, keeping at home anyone who did not have to be out on such a dreadful night. She flicked the reins against Sabra's back, but the old horse had settled into little more than a walk, and Eliza knew the buggy would go no faster. Mercy's farm was just two miles away, but with the time it had taken Davy to hitch up the buggy and Missouri Ann to dress Clara in warm clothing, then bundle her up in a quilt, it would be an hour or more before they reached the Eagles farm. Eliza judged it was already ten o'clock, so she wouldn't return home until past midnight. But as long as she was there before sunup when the Starks were expected, she would be all right.

The buggy wheel hit a rock, and Eliza felt Clara's head bounce against her shoulder and knew the woman was asleep. She wondered how Clara could sleep when her life was in danger, but perhaps she had lived her whole life in fear. Sleep was the best thing for her in her illness, and Eliza was glad the slave could rest. She snuggled up next to Clara and pulled part of the quilt around her shoulders and sank back against the seat. Despite the rain, she felt a kind of peace, as if she were alone in the world. The buggy seemed like a cocoon, and the rain made a sound like soft music. The blackness engulfed her, soothed her, and she felt almost safe.

Eliza thought back to the buggy ride so long ago, when she and Will had ventured out on a rainy day in the Ohio countryside. He had borrowed the buggy from a friend and had showed up at her farm, persuading her father to let Eliza go for a ride, just the two of them. Her father had protested, saying the rain that had come in the morning was liable to return, but Will had pointed to the bright sun and cloudless sky and said that even if the weather turned bad, the buggy had a top that could be raised to keep them dry. The drive had been lovely, past fields of wheat and corn. Goldenrod bloomed on the roadsides as well as asters, and Will had stopped to pick her a bouquet of the purple flowers. They drove farther than they should have, and when the rain came suddenly, it took the two of them to raise the buggy top. The top was cranky, and Will and Eliza were soaked by the time they got it righted.

"I should get you home before you come

down with chilblains," Will said, but Eliza told him the rain was warm, almost like a bath, and she was happy to sit in the buggy until the sun came out. It didn't occur to Will to drive home in the rain anyway, or if it did, he didn't say anything. Nor did Eliza. They sat in the buggy and talked, and then Will reached over and smoothed a wet strand of hair that had fallen across Eliza's face.

"I must look like a drenched chicken," Eliza said, realizing that her hair was plastered to her head, for she had taken off her bonnet when they struggled with the buggy top. She was embarrassed at looking so unsightly.

"You look beautiful. I believe you are the most beautiful young lady in the world," Will said. He had never paid her such a compliment. Indeed, those were words only a lover would utter, and Eliza was embarrassed and turned away, muttering, "Surely not."

Will seemed a little taken aback at his forwardness, but having spoken, he plunged ahead. "I thought you were the prettiest thing I'd ever seen the day I met you, when I wasn't more than ten years old, and I never saw a reason to change my mind. I vowed then I'd marry you, too. Will you have me, Eliza?"

Eliza turned to him, astonished. Not only was her hair damp against her head, but drops of water ran down her face, and her clothes were wet against her body. She had known in her heart that they would marry. There had never been anyone else for either of them. But she had imagined Will would propose in a more formal manner, in her parlor, presenting her with a bouquet of flowers and perhaps getting down on one knee. But she was not a formal person, and the spontaneity of the proposal pleased her. She glanced at the asters he had picked. They were so rain soaked that Will had thrown them onto the ground. The flowers made her laugh, and then she glanced at Will, who had a horrified look on his face.

"I am laughing at the poor flowers and not at you," she said quickly. And then she looked into his kind face, at the blue eyes as bright as a kitten's, his expression expectant, and she reached up and patted his damp curls into place. He looked as bedraggled as she did. "Of course I will have you, Will. If we can pledge ourselves to each other looking our worst, as we do now, I believe we can only look forward to better days."

"My dear one," Will said. He took Eliza's hand and raised it to his lips, and then he put his arms around her and kissed her.

Eliza had never been kissed before, and she wasn't sure it was proper for Will to do so until they were married. What if someone saw them? She glanced around, then laughed again, for who would be spying on them in the rain? And then she boldly raised her mouth and kissed Will.

"We will have a life filled with both sunshine and rain," Will said.

"Sunshine and rain," Eliza repeated, savoring the remark. Later, on their wedding day, she presented him with a quilt she had pieced in a design she had created herself and named Sunshine and Rain. "There are fewer rain squares, because I believe our lives will have more sunshine," she told him, and it had. Will gave her his mother's old wedding ring, worn and thin, promising that one day he would buy her a gold ring with a ruby in it.

"A buggy would be more romantic," she had told him, remembering their ride, and Will had promised that, too.

They had married only a month after Will proposed, and there were those who wondered at the abruptness of the ceremony. But Davy was not born until eleven months later. And then they had taken him to Kansas, not in a buggy, of course—they didn't have one—but in a wagon.

The buggy came later, and it was a surprise. Luzena had been a baby when Will rode Sabra, then a young horse, into Topeka. He had come home to the soddy late at night, long after dark, and he had called, "Come out, come out, Mrs. Spooner. Your husband may take his time, but he keeps his word."

With Luzena in her arms and Davy beside her,

Eliza had opened the door and found Will standing beside Sabra—and a buggy. It was not a new one, of course. Both of them would have considered such an extravagance wasteful. In fact, the buggy had been well used, but it had been finely built and was serviceable. Will had bought it from a man in Topeka whose wife had used it, but she had died, and he no longer wanted it. When Will told him he had long desired a buggy for his wife, the man had replied, "A good wife should not ride in a farm wagon," and had named a fair price.

There had never been a ruby ring. It had become a sort of joke between them, Will promising it for their twenty-fifth anniversary, or maybe their fiftieth. He had mentioned it in one of his letters. Eliza tried to remember which one. She had read his letters over and over again when they arrived, but after his death, she had put them away, saving them to be read at special moments. She wanted the letters to seem new again, to open them as if she were reading them for the first time. And so she had put them into the candle box on the mantel. When Clara was safely gone, Eliza would reward herself by reading one of the precious missives.

She leaned back against the black leather seat, which had cracked in places so that white lines ran from the tufted spots. She was grateful for Will's thoughtfulness in buying the buggy. She and Clara would have been soaked and chilled to their bones in the open wagon. Besides, the buggy was faster—and quieter. The farm wagon could have been heard a quarter mile away in the still night. Davy had removed the bells from the buggy just before Eliza left, and it moved silently in the dark.

Eliza had almost reached the Eagles farm, when she heard horses and a wagon behind her, going fast. In a few minutes, the driver would overtake her. She felt Clara's head rise and knew she had awakened at the sound.

"Mens?" Clara asked.

"I don't know, but best we be cautious. Probably it's a farmer on the road late, or maybe a man out courting." Suddenly, she was afraid. They were two women, one with a price on her head, alone on the dark road. There was no one to look out for her, no man to protect her. A grove of trees loomed up just off the road, and Eliza made for it. The moon was hidden under the clouds, and if they were lucky, whoever was on the road would ride on by without seeing them. Eliza hoped the rain had covered their tracks on the road.

She whipped the reins against Sabra's back and hurried the horse down a lane and into the trees, then stopped under the largest one, whose branches dipped almost to the ground. She jumped out of the buggy and put her hands on the animal's head to quiet her, hoping the scent of the horses on the road wouldn't cause Sabra to neigh. Clara got out of the buggy, too, and came up next to Eliza, saying she would hold the mare. "Get in the buggy, mist'ess, and keep you dry." The rain was falling as hard as ever.

"I am not your mistress, Clara. I am only Mrs. Spooner," Eliza said in a low voice. Then she added, "Maybe you should hide in the ditch or out in the field, just in case someone is up to no good."

"I not leave you alone," Clara said.

"It will be safer for both of us if you do. If there are men looking for you, you will have a chance to get away. The house up ahead, on the left. That is Mrs. Eagles's place. You can explain that I sent you there." She thought a moment, then asked, "Do you know left from right?"

Clara nodded but said, "I stay here to protect you."

Eliza would have none of it and explained that it would go harder on her, too, if slave catchers found her with Clara. She looked around. "The ditch is filled with water, and the fields are too open. Can you climb the tree?"

Clara grinned, the first time Eliza had seen her grin. "Like a squirrel, Miz Spooner."

"It may not be necessary. Wait and see." They spoke in whispers, although the road was a hundred yards away. She whispered to the mare, too, to quiet her, but Sabra caught the scent of the other horses and gave a loud whinny.

The wagon stopped, and a man called, "Who's out there?"

"Hide, then don't move a peg," Eliza whispered, and Clara began to climb the branches. When Eliza looked up, she could not make out the woman's shape. She patted Sabra, hoping the horse would make no further noise, but then the horse whinnied again, and a man called, "Show yourself. I got a gun." The wagon started up and headed toward the trees.

Eliza had no choice. "It's Mrs. Will Spooner," she called. And then she added. "And son."

"Well, Mrs. Spooner, why didn't you say so? I'm Hoyt Wymer out here. What are you doing in them trees?"

"I shall come for you," Eliza whispered, hoping Clara could hear her. Then she got into the buggy, muttering, "Nothing ventured, nothing have," and drove to the man. "Mr. Wymer, you put a fear into me," she said. "I have been sitting with a friend who is ill, and I did not know how late it had gotten. When I heard your wagon, I thought it best to hide. I suppose I am a silly little thing, frightened by the dark." She hoped that the rain had covered up her buggy tracks so that he had not noticed she had been going down the road before him, not toward him.

"You ought'n to be out here. Where's your son?"

"Oh, I just said that, in case you were up to no good."

"You're lucky it's only me. There's slave catchers about."

"Yes, I know. The Starks were at my house and tore it apart."

"That'd be who I'd bet on."

"They found nothing, of course. I don't know who they were looking for."

"A contraband what kilt her mistress, and Starks ain't the only ones out looking. Plenty of men are after that reward."

"How dreadful," Eliza said. "My children will be worried, so I'll be on my way. Give my best to Mrs. Wymer."

"I'd see you to home, but she's ill herself, and I've went to the doctor to get her a tonic. She's waiting for me."

"Then you'd better hurry along. I shall be fine. I have my buggy whip and know how to use it," Eliza said.

"I don't like to leave a lady alone."

"I should not like to delay you when your wife needs you—more than I do."

"There's that."

"Good evening, Mr. Wymer. Tell your wife I shall call with a custard."

"Oh, she'd like that."

Eliza assured him again that she would be all right, and she slapped the reins against Sabra's back and pulled onto the road. And then because she knew Hoyt Wymer was watching her, she turned toward home instead of the Eagles house. She drove until the road turned and she was no longer visible, then pulled to a stop. If the man followed her, she would say the top had slipped and she had stopped to right it. She didn't hear his wagon start up, and that bothered her. She'd also noticed how he'd peered into the buggy as if looking for someone hidden there. Clara would be frightened, left alone in the dark, wondering if Eliza had abandoned her, but it was better to be safe. Eliza would wait until she was sure the farmer was gone. The wind came up and shook the buggy, and Eliza huddled against the seat, thinking if Will were there, he would have taken Clara to Mercy's farm. He would have known how to deal with Hoyt Wymer.

After twenty minutes or so, she heard the creak of a wagon, clear at first, then fainter as it disappeared in the opposite direction. She waited even longer, and then she turned the buggy and went back to the grove.

"Clara," she called softly. "It's Mrs. Spooner. I'm alone."

She did not hear a ruffling in the trees or the sound of footsteps, but in a minute, Clara was beside the buggy. "I hope you didn't fear I'd abandoned you," Eliza said.

Clara didn't reply. Instead, she said, "That man

come over here, walked instead of drove, maybe thinking I wouldn't hear him, and he stay a long time. He call to me, say he come to fetch me to safety, but I know he ain't, and I don't say nothing. He fall in the ditch and get hisself wet, but he don't see me. I hide good." Clara climbed into the buggy and then smiled at Eliza. "He say, 'Damn-fool woman driving in the dark, too purely stupid to hide a yellow dog. Who'd trust her with a slave?'"

The two of them laughed, and Eliza started for the road. "We are going to Mrs. Mercy Eagles's house. You will be safe there, because she has made it known she is not against slavery."

Clara sat up and peered at Eliza in the dark. "Ain't she likely to turn me in to those mens?"

"No, I believe when I tell her your story, she will be as sympathetic as Mr. Ritter and Mr. Hamlin."

Clara stared out into the darkness. "I won't be catched."

"You will be safe. Mrs. Eagles is a good woman."

Clara considered that, but she did not seem persuaded. She moved to the edge of the buggy, as if ready to jump out, and it was clear that she would run if she thought she might be captured. Eliza patted Clara's knee and assured her again that Mercy Eagles was as harmless as a dove.

They pulled the buggy into the Eagles farm,

and left it hidden behind the barn. Eliza was glad to see that despite the late hour, a light shone through the kitchen window, which meant that Mercy was up. She would not have to pound on the door, waking her friend. Eliza could see Mercy sitting at the table, knitting, and went close to the window and called, "Mercy, it's Eliza Spooner."

Mercy jerked up her head as she looked toward the window, and Eliza was sorry she had startled the woman. She thought how frightened Mercy would be alone with two children, and hearing a voice in the night. "It's Eliza Spooner, come on an errand of great importance. Please let me in."

Mercy rose and went to the door, unlatching it. "Eliza, you gave me a fright. What are you doing out in the middle of the night and in all this rain, too?"

"The girls . . . ?"

"Are asleep."

"May I come in?"

"Of course." Mercy opened the door, then stared in shock as Clara followed Eliza into the house. Eliza went to the kerosene lamp and blew it out. "What is going on?" Mercy demanded. "And who is this creature?"

"She is an escaped slave, and I want you to hide her for a day or so."

Mercy put her hand to her chest, her knitting needles thrust upward to her chin, and took a step backward. "Eliza, what are you asking? I'll do no such thing."

"Yes, I believe you will, Mercy, because you are of good character. I would not ask, if Clara's life didn't depend on it. We hid her at our place, but the Starks came today and turned the house and all the outbuildings upside down. It was a miracle she wasn't found. Mother Stark warned us they will be back early in the morning. Clara has been unwell." Eliza thought to ask the slave to show her back to Mercy but would not humiliate her, so said only, "She has been beaten almost to death, the skin flailed off her back. I have never seen such savagery. Her son, a boy not much older than Baby Nance, was whipped to death, and she is accused of killing the person who did the beastly act." Eliza thought it best not to mention that the person was a woman. She explained that John Hamlin had made plans to transport Clara to Colorado, but that the woman had been delirious and unable to travel. She was better now and could continue her journey soon.

"But you know I have never been sympathetic to the cause."

"Yes, that is why your farm is the best place to hide Clara. No one would suspect you."

Mercy thought that over, then shook her head. The children would see her, she protested, but Eliza said Clara could be hidden in the barn for a day. Mercy told Eliza to take Clara to Ettie, whose abolitionist views were well-known. Eliza replied she couldn't, because that was an obvious place to look. In fact, the Starks had already talked about searching the Espy farm.

"Then take her to the sheriff."

"I believe he is proslavery. I'd sooner take her back to my place."

"I can't. I just can't, Eliza. Nathaniel would be furious," Mercy said.

Eliza resisted the impulse to state the obvious, that Nathaniel was dead.

Mercy looked away. "Slavery isn't my fight. I know you think I am wrong, but I'm not an abolitionist. I don't want to be a hero the way Ettie does. I have already given my husband to the war and want no further part of it. Surely you of all people would understand that. I wish the woman well, Eliza, but I can't do as you ask."

Eliza took her friend's hands and waited, while Mercy looked at Clara, then around the room, and finally into Eliza's face. "This is not about slavery, Mercy. It is about a woman, a woman who has been beaten, whose child was murdered. If Clara is captured, she will be smuggled back down South and hanged or maybe consigned to one of those cages that they hang from a tree. I read about them in an abolitionist newspaper. Men will strip her naked and put her into the cage to starve to death, if she doesn't go mad and kill herself first. It is not enough to wish her well. I didn't want to be involved, either, but I didn't have a choice. You don't, either. We are Christian women called upon to do our duty. We must sacrifice as our husbands have. We dishonor them by doing nothing. I believe it will go hard on you for the rest of your life if you refuse Clara. You would not forgive yourself." Then she pleaded, "If nothing else, will you hide her as a favor to me?"

Mercy took a deep breath. Eliza had always thought her a silly thing, but Mercy surprised her as she stood a little straighter and looked Eliza full in the face. "You are right, Eliza. We must accept what we are called upon to do, just as Nathaniel and Will did. I may not agree with you about slavery, but I will not turn away this woman. She can sleep with Mary Ann." She turned to Clara and said slowly and in a louder voice, as if Clara were deaf, "Mary Ann is twelve."

"No need," Eliza told her. "Clara is safer outside the house, and so are you. It is best the children don't know about Clara at all for fear they might say something. Besides, it is not likely, but if someone should come here and find Clara, you can say you were not aware of her presence."

Mercy nodded and offered to fetch a quilt, since the one Clara had was wet, and then the three women walked to the barn in the dark, for they did not want to risk a light. Mercy explained there was a small storeroom behind the hay, where Clara would be safe. Nathaniel had built the hiding place in case Indians came onto the farm, although they never did. After Clara was inside, she and Eliza could pitch hay in front of the door so that no one would know it was there. Eliza asked Clara if she understood, and when Clara nodded, Eliza told her John Hamlin would return the following day.

"The Reverend Hamlin," Mercy said. "So that was what he was doing on your farm the day of the quilting bee. I should have guessed, since I have heard he hid slaves before the war." She led Clara to the little room, no bigger than a wardrobe. It held a broken chair and a trunk whose hinges were dark with rust. "Nathaniel's mother's trunk. She kept her sewing in it," Mercy explained. She forked hay onto the floor to make a bed for Clara. Eliza started to close the door, but Mercy told her to wait. "If Clara is to be here a day or more, she will need something to eat." She hurried back to the house and returned with a loaf of bread, a bowl of cooked potatoes, two boiled eggs, and a jug of water. "I do not dare bring you a candle, for if you caught the hay on fire, you would burn to death. There is no way you could push open the door from the inside. Besides, someone might see the light through the cracks. But in the morning, you will see that daylight comes in, so you will not spend all your time in darkness."

"You give me your needles, I knit. I can knit in the dark," Clara said. "I always be working with my hands. I stitch right good."

But Mercy would not give them up, remarking she had only a single pair. Then she and Eliza closed the storeroom door and piled hay in front of it. When they were finished, Eliza said no one would ever guess there was a hiding place in the wall.

"I believe it will do," Mercy said.

"Why did you agree to it?" Eliza asked, when Mercy walked her to the buggy. The rain had let up, and Eliza paused before climbing into the conveyance.

Mercy smiled. "You are my friend. You asked me. Helping each other is what friends do."

Eliza was exhausted by the time she returned home, unhitched Sabra, and led her into the barn. After she rubbed down the horse, she went to the house and found Missouri Ann in the doorway. "You've not slept?" Eliza said.

Missouri Ann shook her head. "Not till you was home safe. I didn't straighten the house, because likely the Starks'll just tear it up again."

"You are sure they will be here at dawn?"

"I am."

Then they had better get a few hours' sleep,

Eliza said, and the two women lay down on Eliza's bed, fully clothed. Eliza thought she was too agitated to rest well, but minutes after she closed her eyes, she was asleep.

Neither she nor Missouri Ann awoke until they heard mules in the barnyard, and a voice cried, "We know you got the slave girl hid somewheres. Now open the door, or we'll burn down the house and all that's in it. We brung kerosene to help us with the burning."

Eliza righted herself and went to the window, peering out at the sky, which was light in the east. "Will they do it?" she asked Missouri Ann.

"Oh, yes, ma'am."

"Are you ready?"

"I am."

Deciding not to awaken the children, Eliza opened the door and stepped outside. "What are you doing here, Mr. Stark? You have already searched our house and outbuildings. You know no one is hidden here."

"Don't know no such thing. Maybe you hid her before, but I reckon she's right around here now. You probably brung her inside, thinking we wouldn't be back. Well, we outsmarted you." He grinned at Missouri Ann, who stood behind Eliza.

"You've already terrified the children," Eliza said.

"Don't know as I care." He swung down off

his mule, leaving his shotgun attached to his saddle, and gestured to his three sons, who dismounted, too. "I believe we'll start in the house this time, save us trouble. You get in our way and you'll lose an eye. Maybe that girl will, too, the one kept the house bolted up last time. Or maybe you'll get an arm broke off."

"You can't come in here," Missouri Ann said.

"Oh, I can't, can't I? Who's to stop me? Not a puny thing like you."

"I'll stop you," said a voice behind the Starks. "You ain't fit for the kitchen cellars of hell, frightening two women like you just did."

Dad Stark started to turn, but the voice said, "You stay right where you are, Mr. Stark. I have a shotgun trained on you."

Eliza, startled, stared into the darkness, not knowing who had spoken or what the man was doing on her property. Perhaps he was another slave-catcher.

"Who's there?" Dad Stark asked.

"Print Ritter."

Eliza turned to Missouri Ann, who gave her the ghost of a smile. "Mr. Ritter?" she mouthed, and Missouri Ann nodded. "What's he doing here?" Eliza whispered, but Missouri Ann only put her finger over her lips.

"Oh, the fool blacksmith. You spend the night here with Missouri Ann, did you, laying out in the barn like hound dogs coupling?" Dad Stark asked. "Well, you take her for all I care. She ain't good enough for a Stark."

"Watch your mouth," Print said.

"Best you watch yours," Dad Stark said and laughed. "I got three boys with me, and we all got guns."

"Yours is on the horse, and I'll wager the onliest thing your boys have is pistols."

"Good enough to shoot a man. We're four against one."

"Two," another voice said, and Eliza recognized it as John Hamlin's. What were the two of them doing there? she wondered. How had they known about the Starks?

"Oh, a reverend can't shoot worth nothing," Dad Stark said. "He's no more danger than a girl."

"Well, I can shoot," a third voice said.

Eliza could not imagine who that man was, but Dad Stark could. "What you doing here, Tom? You ain't against slavery. We could cut you in on the *re*ward."

The man was the sheriff, Tom Miller. He was proslavery, Eliza knew, so surely he was not there to protect Clara.

"Maybe not," the sheriff replied, "but I sure am against threatening women and children. That's my job. I seen how you tore up the house here and put a fear in those little ones. I knew you was mean, hamfat, but you're even worse'n I thought."

"You got no cause to call me names, Tom. We was just kind of teasing, having a little fun. We didn't mean nothing by it."

"Is that right, Mrs. Spooner?"

Eliza shook her head, then realized that in the dark, the sheriff could not see her. "It is not. He threatened to take my son's arm off, and I believe he would have done it if he hadn't been allowed to go into the house. And you heard him just now, saying he would do the same or even gouge out an eye. Missouri Ann's face is already badly bruised where he hit her, and if you have been inside, you have seen how the Starks tore up the place. A ten-dollar gold piece wouldn't pay for all the damage."

"He threatened to hurt Ma, too," a fourth voice said, and Eliza realized Davy was with the men. She had thought he was asleep in the loft, but he must have gone for John after she left with Clara. He would have run all the way through fields to the Hamlin farm. Then John would have gone for Print and the sheriff. They had come from the opposite direction so Eliza had not encountered them on the road.

"I guess we'll be on our way then," Dad Stark said.

"Not just yet," the sheriff told him. "You ain't leaving less'n Mrs. Spooner says so. You want to charge them with something, ma'am? I'd be happy to jail them."

Eliza thought it over. The Starks deserved to go to jail for the fright they had caused and the mess they had made, but that would make them madder than ever, and despite the sheriff's threat, the Starks might try to get even. Besides, she did not want others to suspect she had hidden Clara. What if John Hamlin needed her assistance again? "I will forgive it this time, but I never want to see a Stark anywhere near this farm. I want their word on it." She wasn't sure why she'd asked that, because the word of a Stark was worthless.

"I'll do better than that. I'll come by here every now and then, and so will Mr. Hamlin and Mr. Ritter, and if we see a Stark within a mile of your farm, I'll make it hot for him. I'll lock him up, and you can charge him then with the mischief he done."

"How'd you know we was coming back?" Dad Stark asked as he mounted his mule.

Eliza feared for Mother Stark, was afraid Dad Stark would whip his wife if he suspected she had warned Eliza. But before Eliza could speak, Missouri Ann said, "I lived with you too long, Dad. I can outsmart a Stark any day of the week."

Later that day, when she was alone in the house, Eliza went to the candle box and took out Will's second letter. She carried it to the bench on the porch so that she could smell the earth scent as she read it. "You would have been proud of me, I think. Oh, how I wish I could have told you about this venture," she whispered as she stared at her name written in Will's hand. And then she added as she unfolded the letter, "But I believe you do know about it. Perhaps it was you who protected us." She looked up at the sky, at a cloud that was long and thin, the sun edging it in gold.

She began to read the letter, but just then, Davy came up and sat down on the porch step. He looked at the letter, and said, "Read it aloud, Mama."

October 18, 1864
Dearest Wife
I do not like the army much. The food is worse than what we feed the hogs. We eat beans & bacon, bacon & beans & crackers so hard you could not break them with a hammer. Yesterday I chewed on a piece of meat that had the hair still on it. Coffee tastes like the runoff from the soddy roof. I would gladly trade my gun for one of your apple dumplings. But I am here in a good cause & should not complain. It is said the Johnnies have it worse. Well, they caused this war & deserve it. I never hated a people so much. If one comes by the farm, you are to take down the shotgun.

Davy made a fist with his right hand and hit the palm of his left. "You should have let me join up, Mama. I could have gotten a Secesh, gotten one for Papa."

"And what if something had happened to you, too?"

"It wouldn't."

Eliza did not remind him that Will had said the same thing. She continued with the letter.

I worry about you & the children living there alone. I have heard terrible things about what some of the soldiers of our own army do to Southern women & can only imagine what the Secesh, the vilest men on earth, would do to a Union woman alone if they were to come into Kansas. Use the shotgun if you have to. But be careful. Guns beg you to fire them.

We ran across a party of Secesh two days ago. War seems to be long days of practice, then an hour or so of the worst excitement I ever saw & we excited those boys pretty bad. There were five of them & I'm sorry to say that three survived, although in poor condition. There is a Southern tradition in this war—I do not know the source of it or what it means—that Johnnies yell to each other, "Mister, here's your mule." We have taken it upon ourselves to say it to the captured Rebs at every opportunity. They do not like it.

Before long you will be harvesting. Do not tax our old horse too much, for she must last at least another year. Davy can help with the plowing, & even Luzena can do her part. If I am not there by spring, do not plant too early, because a frost could scour the tender plants. Those are my orders. Dear me, why do I feel I must instruct a farmer as experienced as yourself? I believe you can do quite well without me, although I do not want your independence to become a habit.

Well, Eliza, that is all I have to say except that I miss you & our children. There is no sight I wish more to see than you standing beside the door as I come up the lane when this terrible war is over. Meanwhile, I think about you every night as I go to sleep. I hope you know how well I love you. Give a great deal of love to Davy and Luzena & save a good measure for "my little girl."

Until I see you, I remain your loving husband
William T. Spooner

Neither Print nor John told Eliza when or how they removed Clara from her hiding place and sent her west. In fact, for all Eliza knew, the escaped slave was still hidden on the Eagles place. But a week later, Mercy Eagles and her children stopped at the Spooner farm on their way to town.

"I've baked a panful of gingerbread and thought I'd share it with you. I remember you liked it, and I thought it would be a nice way to celebrate the end of the war." The news of the surrender had come only two days before. "It came too late for us," Mercy added, "but we must celebrate none-theless."

"We must indeed," Eliza said. "We can be grateful that Ettie's husband will come home now, and Anna's." She did not have to say how sorry she was that Mercy's and her husbands would never come back.

Mercy seated herself on a tree stump and took off her bonnet, using it to fan herself, because the day was warm. She no longer carried her knitting needles. Missouri Ann had cut the gingerbread, and the children had taken theirs out to the orchard. The three women sat in the shade with their cake and talked about the weather, the crops, the promise of more rain. Then Mercy leaned toward Eliza and said, "There is something else." She reached into her basket and removed two folded squares of cloth and handed them to Eliza and Missouri Ann.

Eliza opened hers and found herself looking at a quilt square, but a square like none she had ever seen. The maker had cut out a rough outline of a woman and appliquéd it onto a plain square of fabric. The square had a moon, a tree, and a strange shape that looked almost like a buggy.

She glanced at Missouri Ann's square, which showed a woman and a child. Then she looked up at Mercy, her mouth open. "Clara—"

"I found them in the barn after Mr. Hamlin took her away. There were three. Mine has a woman on it and a barn."

Eliza held the square close so that she could examine it. "I never saw such fine stitching."

"Even better than yours." Missouri Ann smiled. "What will we do with them?"

"They are quilt squares. I shall add mine to a quilt." Mercy looked off into the distance and sighed, then added, "A quilt that will remind me that I must not shirk my duty."

"No," Eliza told her. "It will remind you that when called upon, you did what was right."

"And of our friendship," Mercy said.

Eliza nodded. She would add her square to a quilt, too. Thinking about that she remembered Will's Christmas quilt and wondered again what had happened to it.

CHAPTER EIGHT

April 20, 1865

Anna Bean's hired man, Gage, rushed into Eliza's barnyard in Anna's wagon, whipping the horse, then almost falling out of the wagon when it came to a stop. Gage, old and crippled, had been ill when Anna found him resting against her barn. She'd let him sleep in the hay and had nursed him back to health, although he might have been a fiend who would murder her and the children in their sleep. But Anna had a kind heart, and so did Gage, because when he recovered, he stayed on to help her on the farm, taking his pay in board and room. She was lucky to have him, because well into her pregnancy, Anna could do only a little of the farm work. Now as he rode into Eliza's barnyard, Gage cried, "Come quick, Miz Spooner. She's a-laying there carrying on like I never heard. I went for the doctor, but he's passed out."

"The baby," Eliza told Missouri Ann. "It's not due for another two months."

"Yes, ma'am. She's had her baby come on, and

I ain't never birthed no baby before, not less'n it had four legs."

Eliza called to Luzena to watch over Nance, saying that she and Missouri Ann might not be back until morning. Then, not taking the time to hitch up the buggy, the two climbed into the wagon with Gage and started for Anna's farm. Gage left them there, then hurried on to fetch Mercy and Ettie. Eliza and Missouri Ann hurried into Anna's bedroom and found the woman thrashing about on the bed.

"I don't want to trouble you, but I didn't know who else to send for. Gage says the doctor is senseless from drink, and Mother is in a bad way herself. I don't want a hired man to deliver the baby," Mercy told them between sobs of pain.

"Of course you should have sent for us. What good are friends if you can't call on them in time of need? We'd never forgive you if you hadn't," Eliza said. She asked how long the labor had been going on, and Anna told her since morning. "Best I should take a look and see how far along you are," said Eliza. "I have knowing of this."

Anna nodded, and after examining her friend, Eliza took off her sunbonnet and sat down, saying it would be a while yet.

"I'll boil up some eggshells and have her to drink the water. That'll lessen the pain," Missouri Ann offered. "You put her shoes upside down under the bed to keep her from cramping."

After Missouri Ann left the room, Eliza muttered, "Shoes?" She smiled at Anna, then rose to collect the shoes and place them where Missouri Ann had suggested. "Well, who says it isn't worth a try?"

Anna smiled. The pains had let up, and she rested easier. "I heard if you put an axe under there, it will cut the pain."

"And I heard scissors. My, but it will be awful crowded down there," Eliza said.

Anna reached out and grasped Eliza's hand. Her face was red and her hair wet with perspiration. "I was afraid you wouldn't get here in time, that I'd have to have the baby alone."

"Well, I'm here, and Ettie and Mercy are on their way. Even so, you'd have been all right. I delivered Luzena by myself."

"You did?" Anna asked. She closed her eyes for a moment and dropped Eliza's hand as she dozed off.

Eliza remembered back to that time. Will had told her to ring the dinner bell if she went into labor, and he would come running. She did so, but Will was in the farthest field, breaking rock, and he had thought the faint sound was only the ringing of the sledge on stone. She could have sent Davy for Will, but she thought her husband had heard the bell and would be there at any moment, and so she had spread an old blanket on the table and lay down on it. Her labor with Davy

190

had been short, no more than an hour, and she knew the real birthing pains would come on soon. She prayed Will would get there in time. Davy was on the floor, playing with her saucepan and a ladle, and paid little attention to Eliza's moaning.

When she realized that Will had not heard the bell, she told Davy, "Fetch Papa." She twisted in pain.

The little boy stood up and looked at her. He was only two, but he knew his way about the farm. "Dinnertime?"

"Yes," she said, knowing that would make Davy hurry. "Find Papa. Quick now." She was frightened, because she had lost a half-made baby only the year before.

She watched as Davy went outside, then squatted down to study something on the ground, a bug perhaps, and she called to him to hurry. The pain was bad, and she realized she might have to deliver the baby herself.

When the contraction ended, Eliza climbed off the table and gathered the things she had already put aside for the birthing—clean cloths, a knife, string, a container for the afterbirth, a piece of wood to bite on—and poured water from a kettle resting in the fireplace into a basin, and washed her hands. She set the items on a chair beside the table and lay down again. "Please, God, let him get here before it's too late," she prayed. She couldn't see Davy now, and she hoped the little boy had gone off in search of his father. Then a pain wrenched through her, and she knew the baby was coming.

It was a frightening birth for Eliza, with no one to aid her. She gripped the edge of the table each time the labor pain came, biting her lip instead of the piece of wood, since the stick had been knocked to the floor. She did not want to cry out because Davy might still be about and Eliza did not want to frighten him. There was a great pressure inside her as the baby struggled to be born. Eliza pushed hard, bearing down and grunting, breaking her nails as she clutched the table. Where was Will? What if she could not deliver this baby by herself? What would become of Will and Davy if she failed—and of the baby that tore at her to be born? What if the baby was sideways or was positioned feet first? How could she deliver it by herself?

There was another heaving, and Eliza felt herself stretched to the point she feared she would tear wide open. Frantic, she pushed, taking great gulps of air. And then the baby was out, a tiny wet thing lying on the table, squirming and mewling.

It was over. Eliza let out a deep breath and for just a second lay back on the table, too exhausted to move. She had done it! She had delivered the baby alive, and by herself! Eliza began to cry as she roused herself to cut the cord and tie it. She wrapped the infant in a cloth, then saw to herself. Not until Eliza was finished did she stop to see that the baby was a girl. She had cared only that the birthing had been done right and that both she and the baby were alive.

When all was finished, Eliza swaddled the baby in a cloth and sat down in a rocking chair, examining the tiny hands, the blue eyes with their lashes like bits of thread, the hair that was as soft as a chick's down. Her heart swelled with love—and a little pride.

Will found her there, rushing through the doorway, ducking because Davy was on his shoulders, gasping for breath. Davy had found him, and Will had picked him up and run with the boy. Will stopped when he saw Eliza in the chair, confused, and then he glanced down at the baby and looked again at Eliza with wonder. "Are you—"

"We're fine, both me and your daughter."

"A daughter? A girl?" He grinned. "Well, isn't that fine! I thought it might be a girl."

"A girl or a boy. I thought it would be one or the other."

They smiled at each other, then Will turned to his son. "Look, Davy, what's this?"

"Baby," Davy replied, without interest. He returned to the pan he had left on the floor.

Will picked up the baby and held her, rocking her back and forth in his arms. "What will you name her, Mother?"

"I would like to call her Luzena, for your mother, Lucy, and my mother, Zena. Do you approve?"

"I couldn't think of a better name, except maybe Eliza, but that name is already taken. And I don't believe anyone else could live up to it." He set the baby back in Eliza's lap, and sat down on the floor beside her, and for the first time since she had known him, she saw him weep.

Anna stirred and cried out, biting her lip to keep from screaming. Ettie and Mercy had arrived, and together, they readied the room. They took turns fanning Anna and rubbing her back. Missouri Ann made Anna drink the eggshell water, then went back into the kitchen to prepare some concoction for Anna to drink after the baby arrived. She'd said it was to bring in the mother's milk.

Anna gasped, saying the baby was coming, and the women gathered around her. They had all gone through childbirth, all of them more than once, but they knew that each time seemed like the first, and that Anna was bewildered.

"You forget the pain," Ettie said. "It always surprises you the next time."

"I never saw the need for pain. It ought to be easier," Eliza said.

"Eve's pain," Mercy observed.

"Oh, hush," Ettie told her. "Plenty of men in the Bible did wrong, and men don't get childbirth punishment passed down to them."

The baby came quickly. Mercy took the little girl, while Ettie and Eliza cared for Anna. When they were finished, Anna held out her arms for the baby, who was no bigger than a kitten. "I didn't want her. Up to this morning, I never wanted that baby, but now I think I'd fight a dozen wolves to save her."

"That's the way of it," Eliza said. "You may hate being pregnant, but the minute the baby is born, she is God's precious child, given to you as a gift."

That precious gift was not to be. Eliza volunteered to take the first turn sitting with Anna. The others were preparing to leave when the baby began to cough and then to gasp.

"She's got something in her mouth," Missouri Ann said, putting her finger down the baby's throat, but she found nothing.

"We'll steam her," Ettie said. She put the kettle on. But before the water boiled, the baby took a deep breath and was still. Ettie held the girl by her ankles and spanked her to get her breathing again, but it was no good. The women worked on the baby, but at last, Ettie said, "She was too early. She didn't have the strength to live. We'll have to tell Anna."

But Anna, having heard the commotion in the kitchen, had gotten out of bed and was standing in the doorway. She did not cry out but grasped the back of a chair with one hand and reached for her baby with the other. "Let me hold her." She sat down in the chair and rocked the baby back and forth in her arms, cooing. Her friends gathered around her and waited until Anna relinquished the girl and, without a word, went back into the bedroom and knelt down beside the bed, her head bowed, muttering. Eliza could not tell if Anna was praying or cursing.

The funeral was held the next day. Eliza brought a wooden box not much bigger than a bread pan, lined with her silk shawl, the one she had brought with her from Ohio. Kansas was no place for silk shawls.

So with the Reverend Hamlin presiding, the women buried the baby in the family cemetery, beside the graves of two other children Anna had lost. Gage offered to dig the grave, but the women insisted it was their job, saying it was the least they could do for their friend. The digging didn't take long, because the grave was so small.

As they left the cemetery, Missouri Ann told Eliza, "Maybe it's best. How'd she care for that baby anyway, what with her other'ns and a farm to work?"

"It's never best," Eliza replied. If Cosby Bean did not come back from the war, Anna would grieve even more that the child was lost, Eliza knew. When Will had gone for a soldier, Eliza had been grateful she was not pregnant. But now, with Will gone, Eliza wished he had left behind the start of a baby who would have been a part of himself.

As the women returned to the house, John took Eliza aside and said, "This is not the right place, but what is these days? I would ask if you thought it proper that I call on Mrs. Eagles, even though her husband has not been dead quite a year."

Despite the solemn occasion, Eliza could not help but smile, as she thought that even in the saddest times, there could be moments of happiness. And there would be great happiness if John and Mercy were to join their lives together. She was silent for a moment, as if giving the question great thought. Then she replied, "I believe it would be quite proper. With all that has happened these past years, we cannot be shackled by the proprieties of grieving as we once were. We must take advantage of life, because it is so fragile. You yourself must have seen how Mr. Ritter is already courting Missouri Ann. Widowhood has sorely tried Mrs. Eagles, and I believe she would welcome a chance to enjoy the company of a gentleman."

"I thank you."

Eliza caught sight of Mercy standing in the

doorway, looking out at them, and thought it would not be long before she and John Hamlin were engaged. Even before that, Print Ritter would declare himself to Missouri Ann. That would leave her the only real war widow. But she would not be envious. She would be happy for her friends. There was no man in Wabaunsee County who could measure up to Will. She had had him, and that would be enough.

As Eliza and Missouri Ann started for home, Eliza nodded at John, who was helping Mercy into her wagon. "I expect them to announce their betrothal any day now," she told Missouri Ann.

"You mean . . ."

Eliza nodded. "I am premature, of course, but can you think of a better match?"

"I cannot."

"Me, neither," Eliza told her, "except one."

When Missouri Ann caught Eliza's meaning, she raised her chin and said, "He's just told me he's going to go off to the gold fields, and besides, he ain't asked."

"I hope you would accept if he did. You must not spend your life mourning Hugh."

"I never mourned Hugh," Missouri Ann said hotly. She took a breath to calm herself, then added. "I misspoke. Hugh was a good man."

Eliza studied her friend as they rode along. "What do you mean you never mourned Hugh?"

She glanced back to make sure the children in the back of the wagon weren't listening.

"I said I misspoke."

Eliza shook her head. "I don't believe it. He was not such a good man after all, was he?"

Missouri Ann looked out at a cornfield. The stalks were green, and if the weather was good, the crop would be plentiful. "I want Nance to grow up thinking her father was a decent man, not like the other Starks. She ought'n to think her daddy was evil."

"But he was?" Eliza asked.

"As bad as the rest. He begged me to marry him, but I wouldn't have him. So he held me down and forced me and said he'd make sure I'd have him and nobody else, that nobody else would want me when he was done." She stopped and gave an involuntary sob. "I begged him to stop, but he laughed at me, and he said I was spoilt for anybody else, except maybe his brothers."

"He forced himself? He . . ." Eliza could not say the terrible word.

"That's the truth of it."

"How awful." Eliza wished now that she had not pried.

"When I found out I was in the family way, I didn't have no choice but to take up with him. After we was married, Hugh beat me bad, and sometimes I wished I'd die, but I had to protect my baby. I can't say I purely hate Hugh, because Baby Nance come of it all." She took a deep breath and straightened her back, then turned to Eliza. "I didn't tell you before because I feared you wouldn't take me in. But you've been good to me, so I'm telling you now because you got the right to know what kind of person you brought to your house. You want I should move out now that you know the truth? I wouldn't care to shame you by me being there."

Eliza transferred the reins to her left hand and put her right on Missouri Ann's arm. "My dear friend, it was not your fault, and even if it had been, I wouldn't ask you to leave. As I have said, you are very like a sister to me now. I don't believe I could get along without you."

"You sure have helped me," Missouri Ann said.

Eliza remembered what Mercy had told her the day she'd agreed to hide Clara and said, "And you, me. Helping each other is what friends do."

It wasn't more than a week before Print Ritter rode into the barnyard where Eliza and Davy were shelling walnuts and tied his horse to the rail. He wore a clean shirt, and Eliza thought that while he was not as handsome as Will, he was nonetheless a fine-looking man.

"May I have a minute, Mrs. Spooner?" he asked, taking off his hat. He glanced at Davy, who stood and said it was time to start the milking.

"You are welcome to sit down, Mr. Ritter, although I expect you've come to see Missouri Ann, who is in the house."

"Yes, ma'am." He waited until Davy had gone into the barn, then leaned forward. "I come to talk to you on a serious matter."

Eliza was puzzled and told him to go ahead.

"I would like to ask your permission for Mrs. Missouri Ann's hand in marriage."

Eliza almost whooped, for the idea that she held sway over Missouri Ann tickled her. "Ask *me?*"

"Yes, ma'am."

"She is her own person, Mr. Ritter. She will make the decision without my help."

"Well, I feel it's proper to ask somebody, and none of the Starks is going to say yes. It's not right, her being a lady, that I shouldn't ask. I aim to take her to Colorado, if she'll have me."

"And Nance, too?"

"Yes, ma'am. She ain't likely to go without that baby." He paused. "Nor me, neither."

"No, I can see your point." Eliza pretended to ponder Print's question. "If it is up to me to allow you to marry Missouri Ann, then I will ask you to promise to cherish her and care for her and never raise a hand to her."

"That's an easy promise."

Eliza wondered if Missouri Ann had told him about the rape, and if she hadn't, what Print's

201

reaction would be if he found out, whether he would still want her. Of course, it was not Eliza's place to reveal Missouri Ann's secret. Nonetheless, she said, "Missouri Ann is a good woman, the finest I've ever known. She has had a hard life, harder than most, and been ill treated—"

"I know that, Mrs. Spooner. She informed me of the circumstances of how she come to marry a Stark, and I think highly of her for telling me. It wasn't her fault. If I was to meet up with Hugh Stark, I'd punch him in the nose for what he done to her, but I guess I can't sock him on account of he's dead."

"No." Eliza smiled and dusted the bits of black walnut shell off her hands. "Then you have my approval, Mr. Ritter, but only if Missouri Ann says yes." She paused. "I have no doubt as to her answer."

Print grinned at Eliza, then went to the house and knocked on the door. A few minutes later, he came out with Missouri Ann, who said, "Me and Mr. Ritter's going to take a walk to the orchard."

Eliza nodded and tried to look casual, glancing down at the black walnuts that remained to be cracked, although she knew she was too excited now to deal with them. She watched as Print took Missouri Ann's arm and the two of them disappeared among the apple trees. Davy came from the barn then, just in time to see the couple leave. He grinned at Eliza and said, "It's about time he asked her to marry him."

Davy went back to his chores, but Eliza sat on the bench until dusk waiting for Print and Missouri Ann to return. When they did, they were holding hands, Print grinning and Missouri Ann looking flustered and happy. "You'll never guess what Mr. Ritter gave me," Missouri Ann said.

"Why, I can't imagine."

"He gave me a proposal of marriage."

"What a surprise," Eliza said.

"We're going to find a gold mine in Colorado, and maybe one day we'll come back to Kansas and buy us a farm. I wouldn't want to leave Kansas for good. I believe it's as close to heaven as I'll ever get." She smiled shyly and added, "Especially if Mr. Ritter's here."

CHAPTER NINE

May 4, 1865

Both Print and Missouri Ann wanted to be married as soon as possible. The war had ended a month before, and soldiers would be heading west to find gold mines. Print hoped to beat them to it. Besides, Missouri Ann had run into Taft Stark in town the week before, and he'd told her that Mother Stark was ailing and wanted to see Nance. It would be a kindness if she would call with Nance, he'd said. But Missouri Ann remembered Mother Stark's warning about visiting and refused to go. What if the Starks claimed the baby? Missouri Ann was scared, especially after Taft told her that a lawyer had informed them they had a right to Hugh's child. If the Starks knew she was going to be married, they'd say that she could have other babies and that Nance belonged to them.

So Print and Missouri Ann decided to be married right away. They would keep the wedding a secret, even from the other three members of the quilting circle. The women would be hurt if they weren't invited to the ceremony, hurt that they couldn't use a bit of their hoarded sugar and cinnamon to make cakes and pies to honor their friend. But Missouri Ann couldn't risk the chance the Starks would find out.

The day before the ceremony, Ettie showed up at the Spooner farm with a chocolate cake, filled with nuts and dried fruit. "It's what you'd call a groom's cake," Ettie explained. "Not that there's any need for one, you understand. I just made it and thought you might like it, seeing as how the war's done with, so it's a reason to celebrate."

Ettie didn't fool Eliza. "How did you know about Missouri Ann?" Eliza asked.

The older woman flipped her hand back and forth. "Know what?"

Eliza only smiled at her, inviting Ettie to explain herself.

"Mercy and Anna haven't heard a thing about it. So don't you worry. By the way, it's been rumored in town that Print's going off to California if they marry. Amos Stark asked if that was so, and I told him he best not let the rest of his family know. Colorado, is it?"

Eliza wouldn't answer. She didn't have to. She knew full well that Ettie had all the details.

"Lord Harry! I'll miss that girl. She's like a bit of yellow silk in an overalls quilt, makes you smile when she speaks. I believe she's as good a friend as you'll ever have, Eliza."

"She is at that," Eliza replied. She didn't know what she'd have done without Missouri Ann and her other friends, who had held on to her in her time of sorrow. One of them was always stopping by with a custard sprinkled with a rare bit of cinnamon or a bottle of peaches or a jar of pickles, saying, "I just don't have a taste for them right now." They shared their scraps of fabric with her. Mercy loaned her a book of poems. Anna brought a little framed picture she had composed of pressed flowers. But mostly, they came to sit with her, to spend an hour or two to keep her from loneliness. Eliza knew what it took to snatch the hours away from chores, and she was grateful most of all for their presence. Without friends, she could not have made it through the first days of that hard time. She did not want to think how lonely she would be without Missouri Ann.

"I'll just be on my way," Ettie said, "but I believe I'd like to see Baby Nance one more time." Ettie went outside and cornered Missouri Ann and Nance, and Eliza saw Ettie embrace them both.

Missouri Ann came into the house, shaking her head. "I suppose it's not a surprise me and Print are getting married, but how did she know it was tomorrow?"

"Ettie always knows. But she'll keep it to herself."

"That Ettie. She's a daisy."

The wedding was even simpler than Eliza's own wedding, which had been performed in the parlor of her parents' house in Ohio, with only family and a few friends in attendance. Now, as she stood up with Missouri Ann as Print and Missouri Ann said their vows, Eliza thought back to her own wedding day, in late spring when the smell of lilacs drifted through the windows and birds sang in the meadow beyond the house. She was dressed in pale green lawn, a white ribbon for a sash, which emphasized her tiny waist. Her white kid slippers barely showed under her skirt, which was made of yards and yards of material and was full over her hoops. She carried a bouquet of daisies. Eliza and Will had stood in front of the parlor window, the breeze blowing the curtains, making them billow just like Eliza's wedding skirt. She remembered how after he slipped the old ring onto her finger, Will kept hold of her hand and would not let go, held it until the end of the ceremony. He squeezed so hard that Eliza's blood almost stopped. Will had teased Eliza that he would kiss her at the end of the ceremony, and Eliza almost hoped he would, although such a thing would have been unseemly and would have shocked the guests. But Will held his kisses until they were alone.

When the ceremony was over, Eliza's father recorded the names and date in the family Bible, then her mother set out refreshments—a cake, lemonade, and the divinity candy whose recipe had been passed down for generations and was served only on special occasions. Afterward, the couple climbed into a borrowed buggy and set out for the farm Will had rented. They lived there until they moved to Kansas.

Eliza recalled her wedding night. She had grown up on a farm. She knew what happened between male and female, but she was a little afraid of the act, not sure what was expected of her. After all, some of the male animals were violent when they mated. She wished her mother had told her, but Eliza's mother was prim. So were her married girlfriends. They said only, "It's not so bad. Wait and see." Will was gentle, kind, saying he would stop if she wanted him to. But she didn't, partly because she was curious, partly because she wanted it over with. There was no joy in the act for her that night, but it came later. Now as she listened to Print and Missouri Ann recite their vows, with John Hamlin officiating, Eliza grieved for the pleasure that was no longer hers, would never be hers again.

Just as John pronounced Print and Missouri Ann man and wife, there was the clatter of horses and a wagon in the lane, and Eliza feared that the Starks had found out about the wedding and meant to stop it. If they had, they were too late. Instead of the Starks, however, Ettie drove into the barnyard, Mercy and Anna on the seat beside her, the children in the wagon bed.

"I know the wedding is a secret, but by morning, it won't be anymore," Ettie said. "Mercy and Anna would flail me alive if they found out I knew Missouri Ann was getting married and hadn't told them. We're your friends, and we're here to celebrate with you." Eliza was glad they had come, not just because her friends would blame her for keeping the secret but because their presence underscored how much they valued Missouri Ann. The woman had had few friends since she'd married Hugh Stark, and those friendships with the members of the little quilting group were something she could savor all her life.

Ettie climbed down from the wagon with a bundle covered with white muslin. "I expect you could use another quilt out west, it being cold as a widow's bed there," Ettie said, then put her hand over her mouth, glancing at Eliza and Mercy. "I shouldn't have said that. I ask you to forgive it. I open my mouth before I think."

"This is a day for happiness," Eliza told her, and Mercy agreed.

Ettie nodded. "I brung you a quilt, Missouri Ann. We all worked on it, even you, so it's a gift from all of us." She unfolded a pieced quilt.

"It's your Kansas Dugout," Missouri Ann said. "Isn't that the sweetest thing! Why, that means we'll always sleep in Kansas."

"I thought you might feel that way. It'll serve until you come back home," Ettie told her, looking pleased with herself that the gift was a success.

"I never got a present before, and now I have two," Missouri Ann said, flustered. "Look what Print give me." She held out her hand to show off a gold ring with a clear stone in it. "I never had a ring before. It's got glass in it."

Anna grasped Missouri Ann's hand so they all could admire the ring. "I believe that's a diamond," she said.

"What's that?"

"It's a stone."

Missouri Ann frowned, then whispered, "Don't say nothing to Print about that. Leastways the diamond's as pretty as glass."

Eliza served Ettie's cake and her own white cake topped by whipped cream, and then as the guests wished them a happy life, Print and Missouri Ann climbed into Print's wagon and were off. Print had sold the smithy to Andy Jones for more than enough to make the trip.

"We'll be back. We ain't going to Colorado for all time. We're Kansas people," Missouri Ann called, as the wedding party followed the couple down the lane. Print slapped the reins over the horses, Missouri Ann held on to his arm, and Nance perched beside her, clutching Miss Cat, Luzena's doll. Luzena, saying she herself was too old for dolls, had presented it to Nance as a remembrance.

Eliza and the others stopped at the main road and watched until the wagon disappeared. "I was never happier to perform a wedding," John said, as he stood in the dust. He took Mercy's arm as they walked back to the house, and Eliza knew there would be another wedding before long. Of all the members of her quilting group, only she would be without a husband. And suddenly, Missouri Ann's wedding day became the lone-somest day Eliza ever saw.

The Wabaunsee County men began returning home. Ettie's husband and son rode into the Espy farm one morning, the man whole but the boy weak in mind. He'd seen too much savagery, Ettie explained to Eliza. Cosby Bean came back, too. Not long after Missouri Ann's wedding, Eliza went to the Bean farm to present Anna with a washboard she had found lying in the road. It must have fallen from a wagon passing through and would be sorely missed. But it had been Eliza's good luck to find it, and as she had a serviceable washboard herself, she thought to give it to Anna, whose own board had worn through. As the two women stood talking in the kitchen of the Bean house, they glanced out the window to see a man in a ragged Union uniform on the road. Anna sighed and asked,

"Will they never stop coming, those poor men?"

"They fought to keep the country together, and now they are let go as if they are of no more consequence than a used-up horse. You stay, Anna. I'll see if he wants a drink of water." Anna still suffered from childbirth, and the farm work taxed her. Eliza went outside and stood on the stoop and watched the man turn into the dirt lane to the house. She started forward to offer him a drink, but suddenly, she stopped and called, "Anna, come quick."

Anna stepped outside the door. "What . . ." She stopped and froze for a moment, and then she flew down the lane, her arms wide, calling, "Cosby, Cosby." She all but jumped into his arms, and the two held each other for a long time. Eliza could see the sheen of tears on both faces. They walked slowly to the house, their arms around each other, and Anna said, "It's Cosby! Cosby's come home!"

"I can see that," Eliza said.

Anna's two little boys heard the commotion and ran outside, then stopped, looking at their father in awe, and Eliza realized they did not know who he was. "Your papa," she whispered.

"Papa?" the younger one asked, as if he didn't know what the word meant. But the older one did and he looked at Cosby shyly.

Anna held out her hands to the boys, and they came to her. And then Cosby grabbed them up.

He carried them to the house, past Eliza, who wondered if, in his joy, he hadn't even noticed her.

"Eliza . . ." Anna began, but Eliza shook her head.

"I'm so glad, Anna. It's a time for your family."

Anna nodded and followed her husband into the house and closed the door, while Eliza went to her buggy and untied Sabra. She *was* glad for Anna, Eliza thought. She would not dwell on why her friend's husband had come home and hers had not. She thought to call on Mercy then, since Mercy's husband, like Will, would never return. But Mercy was being courted by John now.

"Oh, Will!" Eliza cried, as she climbed into her buggy. "Why wasn't it you? Why weren't you the one to come home?" The loneliness was terrible. Eliza thought she might die of it, this needing of her husband. When she arrived home, she put the horse in the corral and then went inside and took down the candle box where she kept Will's letters and removed one. She had read it when it arrived at the post office. The final letter, of course, had never been opened. She could not read that one yet, perhaps not ever.

October 30, 1864
My Beloved Wife
I am sick of this war & tired, very tired. We have marched long & late, from sunrise until

5 in the evening, went two miles on the wrong road & had to turn back & retrace our steps. Now I have thrown myself on the ground determined to write to you before I fall asleep. We were lucky to forage a few potatoes from a farmhouse & that kept me going. May the Lord God forgive me for breaking His commandment. I hope He knows I steal only to keep body & soul alive. Surely He is a Yankee & understands. I believe He must despise the Confederates as much as I do.

The only thing that sustains me is knowing you & Luzena & Davy are safe at home, away from this cruelty & death. Many escaped slaves have come into our camp, & you would be disheartened to hear their stories. Be grateful you are too far away to encounter them.

Eliza smiled to herself. If only Will had known. But maybe he had. Maybe it was Will who had watched over her in the rain on that dark night with Clara.

I have not much to tell. We tramp & tramp & then we engage the enemy & for an hour or two, we live in terror. The dirt & smoke are so thick in battle that we do not know if we are shooting foe or friend. May God have mercy if I have murdered one of my comrades. In the last engagement, the man fighting next to me was felled by a bullet from behind. He had raised up his head at the wrong moment & was killed by a Union soldier. Had I been a little closer, I might have gotten the bullet. Never fear, dear wife, I am disposed to keep my head down. A Secesh had me in his sights that same day, but I laid him aside. It was a bad fight. The bushes were chawed off by the bullets, not a leaf was left. When all was done, the bodies of the dead were covered by a network of twigs & leaves. The dead are placed in trenches & covered by soil, the way I cover the potatoes to protect them from the frost of winter. Often our men are buried in bunches, like dead chickens. Sometimes the graves are so shallow that the wild hogs dig up the bodies & consume them. The people hereabouts refuse to eat the pigs.

We barely have time between battles to rest but must be on our feet to march again. Time marches on even faster. I thought it was only mid-October but am told the month is nearly over. Still, time cannot move fast enough for me. We have been ordered to lay by a day, then take the town, but God bless me, I do not know what town that is.

I have the picture of you taken just before I went for a soldier. You are wearing the blue dress, your hand with the old wedding ring at your throat, & it reminds me I never bought you the gold ring with the ruby. I intend to do it first thing I return. I hope you are getting on well—but not too well—without your old husband.

Now, Eliza, I forbid you from working too hard. You will do the children no good if you are not fit because of overwork. But I would like to ask you to knit me some mittens, if it is not too much trouble. We received a shipment of them made by Quaker ladies, but they are worthless, as they were knit without trigger fingers. You would laugh were you to see some of the items made by wives. One sent her husband velvet slippers with roses embroidered on them, while another made a pair of trousers that button on the wrong side. The soldier must stand on his head to button them.

Scurvy has broke out & I wish you could send me a sack of onions. We don't eat so good now. Last night all I had was ramrod bread, which is cornmeal smeared on my rifle ramrod and cooked over a fire.

Eliza had sent the onions. She'd made the mittens, two pairs, and a muffler, too, but Will had never written of their arrival. She wondered what had happened to them.

I have never been so weary. I would trade a week's rations for one good night's sleep. If it were not for the bugle or the kicks of the officers to send us on our way, I believe I could sleep for a month. I have not shaved since I left home & must carry five pounds of dirt in my beard and clothes. My appearance would make a cat laugh.

Forgive me for writing such a sorry letter. If I could not unburden myself on you, I do not think I would make it. I know this war is not easy for you, either & that you endure hardships you do not tell me about. Dearest Eliza, I push on to finish off this war. I feel it will end soon & I will rejoin my family & friends in Kansas ere long.

Remember me to the children. Give them love from their old Papa & keep a good measure of it for yourself.

Your Devoted Husband
William T. Spooner

In June, the Starks left Wabaunsee County. Nobody knew for sure where they had gone, but several noted that when they left, the Starks headed south. And later on, a man passing through remarked about a family of surly men he'd encountered on his way from Texas.

Because he held the mortgage on the farm, John Hamlin claimed the Stark house and land, which was foul with refuse and dead animals and a mule in such poor condition that it had been left in the barn to starve. John brought it to Eliza and said if the animal was cared for properly, it would heal and could be hitched to a plow. "It would be a kindness to one of God's creatures if you'd take it in," John said.

Eliza saw through the ruse. John was like Eliza's other neighbors, who under the pretext of asking her for a favor were doing her a good turn. She did not have the money for a mule, and Sabra was too old to work much in the fields. John knew that and was giving her the mule in such a way that her pride would not be hurt. Eliza accepted the animal in the manner in which it was presented. Perhaps John should have given the mule to the man who let the Stark farm, but Eliza was in such need that she didn't suggest it. The new tenant was a one-armed Union veteran named Root who would work the place with his twin boys, Chad and Cheed. The man's wife, John mentioned, had hung quilts on the wall, quilts almost as pretty as Eliza's. She understood that John expected her to return his kindness by calling on Mrs. Root and becoming her friend. Eliza would do that.

And she would care for the soldiers, just as she hoped someone would have cared for Will if he'd needed it. Eliza was used to seeing bummers and Union soldiers tramping along the road on their way west. Some bore wounds. Others had soldier's heart, the weariness that came from seeing too much death and carnage. A few rode horses but most walked. Sometimes they stopped at the farm and asked for water or begged a meal, and Eliza, knowing Will would have wanted her to, shared her supper or even went without to give it to the hungry men. A few inquired about work, but Eliza could not pay them. On occasion, a soldier, asking nothing more than a little food and a place in the barn to bed down, stayed a day or more and worked the fields or repaired the barn or mended harness. The familiar work took his mind off the terrible war, he would say. But after a time, each of them moved on.

The last one had disappeared the day before a man Eliza thought never to see again rode into the Spooner farm.

CHAPTER TEN

July 2, 1865

The afternoon had been hot, and Eliza had taken a resting spell under the cottonwoods that lined the creek. She and Will had fished the creek on summer afternoons, never catching much more than crawdads, but they didn't mind, because it was peaceful in the shade. They had been lucky to find land with a grove of trees. The creek was Eliza's favorite place on the farm, and she couldn't help but think of Will as she sat on the bank with her bare feet in the water.

Was it only the summer before that Will had caught her like that? He had crept up and howled like an Indian, and Eliza had been so startled that she fell into the creek. She was furious at her husband, who laughed at her as he reached down to help her climb the bank. "How could you!" Eliza cried, and then she yanked Will's arm, and he, too, fell into the water. He looked so comical as he stood up, water dripping from his head, his clothes soaked, his hat floating on the water, that she forgot she was angry and began to laugh. They both laughed.

"I can't work in wet clothes," Eliza said, removing her dress and hanging it on a tree branch in the hot sun. Will took off his shirt and pants, too, then suddenly turned and grabbed her up. He lowered her onto the ground, and they made love. Right there, in the daylight, on the ground, not even thinking someone might come upon them.

The memory made Eliza flush, and sitting under the trees alone, she thought this a sacred place. She felt Will's spirit and wished she had brought one of his letters with her. The remembrance of Will brought her pleasure then, not pain, and Eliza wondered if that was a change in her, if from now on Will's life and not his death would be foremost in her mind. Perhaps the joy would come only once in a while, but it was a start toward acceptance.

Eliza would have stayed there all day, but there was work to be done. So she walked back across the fields to the barnyard and was startled to find a man there sitting on a horse, his back to her.

"I say again, hello the house," he called in a harsh voice. That was the proper thing for a stranger to do, to wait in the yard until someone came out to greet him. He was a large man with a beard the size of a rosebush, and his horse was a fine one. If he was a soldier, he was no ordinary soldier.

He did not see Eliza as she emerged from the field behind him. She saw him look around the farm as if it were his, and she thought him a little arrogant. Because of the horse and the rider's fine suit of clothes, she wondered if he was an officer, and then she noticed the gray cape and decided he was a Confederate. She would offer him a drink, but she would not give him a meal. She hoped Davy was not around. Since he hated the Secesh as much as Will had, he might start a quarrel. When the man saw her, he made no move to dismount or even remove his hat.

"There's a dipper by the well," Eliza said.

"Didn't come for water."

Eliza waited.

"I said I didn't come for no water."

"Then what is it I can do for you, sir? Why are you here?"

The man threw his leg over his horse and looked around the farm again, peering at the house and then the barn. He studied Luzena as she came outside and threw a pan of dishwater into the flower bed, stared at her as if he had the right. "I come looking for someone."

"There is no one here to interest you. I believe you may have gotten the wrong farm."

"Oh, I got the right farm." He slowly dismounted and stood before Eliza. "I got the right farm, Eliza Spooner."

Eliza stared at the man. The beard covered his face, but his eyes were familiar—dark eyes, deep, maybe cruel. She did not like them. "Who are you?"

"Don't you know?"

Eliza shook her head.

The man gave a mirthless smile and said, "I'm Hugh Stark, and I come for my wife."

"Hugh!" Eliza's hand flew to her mouth. "But you're dead. I saw the letter."

"Oh, I wasn't dead. I just didn't want to be a soldier no more." He chuckled as if he had just shared a joke.

Eliza stared. "How can that be?"

"I put my truck on a dead Yank, and I give a man a dollar to make sure the gov'ment thought I was the one that was dead. Then me and another fellow took off. You heard of Quantrill?"

Eliza had indeed heard of the outlaw who terrorized Kansas with his gang of bushwhackers. They sympathized with the South and were no better than thieves and cutthroats. "You were one of Quantrill's Raiders? But you enlisted for the Union."

"I never cared about the Union. Nor the South, neither, if you want to know the truth of it. I just wanted to get off the farm, and I had me a gaysome time of it. But I come back for Missouri

223

Ann, so you tell me where's she at. And you be quick about it. I ain't got time to waste. They say there's a price on my head for what I done with Quantrill, so ain't nobody in Wabaunsee County to know I'm here."

"What makes you think Missouri Ann is with me?"

"Oh, I come across Dad and them down south of here. Funny thing running into them like that, right there on the road. They thought I was dead. Missouri Ann done a good job of telling it. Why, they was never so happy to see a body as they was to see me. Mother even said it was like the resurrection of Jesus Christ." He paused, thinking that over. "I guess it was at that." He smiled, and Eliza thought there was never a man so unlike Jesus Christ as Hugh Stark. And one who so little deserved resurrection.

"At any rate, Amos said Missouri Ann'd been living with you, but he believed she had married the blacksmith, damn her soul. I went to the smithy, but it's been sold. Missouri Ann shouldn't have done that. She should have acted like a proper widow, waiting for her husband to come back."

Eliza blinked at the irrationality of what he'd said.

"You know as well as me that marriage ain't legal, me being her real husband and alive and all. Mother says to leave be, that there's plenty of girls younger and prettier who'd have me. But I fancy Missouri Ann. Besides, she belongs to me, and ain't nobody else going to have her." He looked at the house, but then turned back to Eliza and stared at her with his angry eyes.

"Missouri Ann believed you were dead. She had a right to marry again. You leave her alone. She's found a better man than you."

Hugh smirked. "Ain't nobody better than me, not for Missouri Ann anyway."

"Oh, I know about you, Hugh Stark. Missouri Ann told me how you held her down, forced your seed into her." Eliza blushed at words that burned her tongue.

"I didn't force nothing on her. She wanted it. She's a wildcat, that one. Hell, I might not even have been the first one. If Nance hadn't looked so much like a Stark, I'd of thought she might not be mine."

"How foul!" Eliza shouted. "You profane her. You have no right."

Eliza was so loud in her declaration that Luzena came outside and walked toward her mother, a carving knife in her hand. "You want me to ring the bell, Mama?" she asked. The bell would summon Davy.

"That isn't necessary. Mr. Stark is just leaving." Eliza feared that with his quick temper, Hugh might find a reason to attack Davy, and she knew Starks fought dirty.

At the name Stark, Luzena jerked up her head, then moved to her mother's side. "Which Stark?" she whispered.

"*Hugh* Stark. He wasn't dead after all, just a common deserter," Eliza replied.

Hugh smirked, then looked over the girl, grinning at her. "You're just about the size of Missouri Ann when I first knowed her—knowed her like the Bible says."

Eliza clenched her jaw. "You'd best be on your way, Hugh. We do not care to have you here."

He laughed, then took a step forward, towering over Eliza and Luzena. "Now you tell me where Missouri Ann's at or maybe I'll just take this girl. She looks ripe enough."

Luzena looked up at her mother, then slowly moved her hand to give Eliza the knife. But Hugh saw the weapon, and before Eliza could grasp it, Hugh brought his huge hand down on her arm, and the knife fell to the ground.

"Mama!" Luzena screamed, grasping her mother's arm, but Hugh yanked her away, dragging her toward the horse. Eliza rushed forward, as Luzena whimpered, "Don't let him take me."

"Let her go!" Eliza screamed, but Hugh only laughed and tightened his grip on Luzena's arm.

"Help me, Mama," Luzena cried.

"You tell me where Missouri Ann's at?"

"I won't," Eliza replied.

Hugh twisted Luzena's arm until she screamed and cried, "Tell him Missouri Ann went off to Oregon. It doesn't matter. It's a big territory. He'll never find her."

Hugh laughed as he released Luzena, shoving her to the ground, and turned to Eliza. "Well, now, I guess I got what I come for. I'd take this one with me, but she's not woman enough for a Stark. I'll tell Missouri Ann when I catch up with her that you said howdy. She'll say it back, that is if I let her."

"No, Hugh, you mustn't go there," Eliza protested. "She has a new husband, a good one. Shame on you for following after her."

Hugh mounted his horse, and pulled back on the reins so hard that the horse took a step backward. "Mother fancies that baby. Maybe I'll bring Nance back instead of Missouri Ann." He spurred the horse and took off down the lane.

Luzena lay in the dirt until Hugh was gone, then Eliza helped her stand. "Is your arm all right?"

"I screamed louder than necessary."

"You were a brave girl," Eliza said.

"He wouldn't have taken me, would he?"

"No." But Eliza wasn't so sure. "Whatever made you smart enough to say Missouri Ann had gone to Oregon?"

"It was all I could think of. I couldn't say Colorado. I guess I can outthink a Stark."

"You do it even better than Missouri Ann." Eliza paused a moment. Then she said, "Luzena, I believe it is best that we don't tell anyone about this, even Davy. Mr. Stark said it's not known he has been here, so no one but us will be aware he is alive."

"But what about Missouri Ann?"

"She should know least of all. You see, since Mr. Stark is alive, Missouri Ann is still married to him. That means she is . . ." She paused, but continued when she decided that Luzena was old enough to understand. "She is living in sin with Mr. Ritter. But if she does not know it, is she really living in sin? I believe the knowledge Hugh is alive would only bring her grief. Can you keep the secret?"

Luzena smiled at her mother. "You know I can."

They never heard of Hugh Stark again, or any of the Starks, for that matter. People believed they had settled in Texas or perhaps had gone on to Arkansas or Alabama. But at any rate, they disappeared from Wabaunsee County.

Some weeks later, Eliza received a letter printed in a childish hand that she recognized immediately as Missouri Ann's. Eliza had picked up the letter at the post office and put it into her basket so that no one would see it. She believed it prudent to keep Missouri Ann's whereabouts to only the members of the quilt group. Outside, she stood by herself in the sun, too excited to wait until she returned home to read the letter. So using her fingernail, she picked at the wax on the envelope and removed the letter, noting as she did that the envelope was postmarked Georgetown, Colorado Territory.

Dear Friend Eliza

Me & Print Ritter & Nance has arrived in Colorado & we are living in the mountains. Print & his brother are looking for a gold mine. I like Print fine but I don't like mountains. They are too big. Print says when we get our stake we will go back to Kansas, that is if the Starks has gone off. I ain't so much afraid of them out here. You will never guess who I saw when we went through Denver. It was Clara the colored we hid. She made it safe & she takes in laundry. She come right up to me on the street her not even knowing who I was & says in the funny way she talks you got washing you need done lady? Well, I says you look like Clara & she says I am Clara & I say I'm Missouri Ann & I'm married now & I'm Mrs. Ritter. She did my washing & didn't charge a cent. She says if you come to Colorado she'll do yours free too because you was so good to her. She asked what you done with the quilt square & I told her mine was right there with me in the wagon but I didn't know nothing about what you done with yours. Well we are fine. Nance talks a good bit now & next year me & Print have got up our own baby. I am sorry I left you when you was grieving so bad & I hope you are better. Please write to your old friend & tell me the news. Print says to give Mrs. Spooner his regards & regards from your friend Missouri Ann, too.

Mrs. Print Ritter that was Missouri Ann Stark

As Eliza folded the letter and placed it back in the envelope, she thought about the child that Missouri Ann would have, and it struck Eliza then that life didn't stop. Will was dead, but Missouri Ann was going to have a baby. Birth and death were God's way, she told herself. Joy and sorrow were joined together.

Missouri Ann's letter reminded Eliza of the quilt square depicting a woman and a buggy that Clara had left for her. So after she returned home, Eliza removed the square from her sewing basket and took it and her scrap bag outside, where she sat on a stump and thought how she would incorporate the square into a quilt. She could use it as the center block of almost any design. Or perhaps she would make one of the Album quilts she had read about in *Peterson's Magazine*. She could make other squares depicting the barn, the fields, the church, the children, her quilt group. As she reached into her scrap bag to see what other colors she had, Eliza peered through the thick trees that hid the farm from the road, and glimpsed a man. She wouldn't have paid much attention except that he was going east along the road instead of west. Most of the soldiers headed west, so perhaps he was a settler returning to his farm.

Although it was midsummer, they still came, those discharged men. In the beginning, they had been strong-bodied, but the ones who stopped now were often the sick ones, lame, held up by friends, all of them headed for home, or maybe a better life somewhere to the west.

This man was tall and walked with a limp, and Eliza thought he would go on past, but he stopped and stared at the house for a long time before he turned down the lane. It crossed Eliza's mind as it had every time a soldier passed now that maybe he was Will. If Hugh Stark could come back from the dead, why couldn't her husband? But Will was no deserter. Besides, she could tell from the shape of the man that he was no one she knew. A sadness still came over her each time she saw a soldier and knew he was not her husband.

Eliza stood and walked to the well as the man reached the barnyard. He would want water. Maybe she'd invite him to supper, that is, if he was a Union man. She couldn't tell from his clothes.

As the man reached her, Eliza saw that he was not just thin but emaciated, his cheekbones protruding as if his face were only skin and bones. She thought she would at least offer him a little bread. "The water bucket's on the side of the well, and there's a dipper," she said. "How long since you ate?"

"Thank you, ma'am. It's been more than a day, and months since I had what you'd call a meal."

From the man's way of speaking, Eliza knew he was a Southerner.

He lifted the dipper from its hook and took a fulsome amount of water, drinking it down. He filled the dipper a second time and drank. Then he replaced the dipper and turned to Eliza. "Would this be the Spooner farm?"

Eliza was taken aback. Why would a Confederate be asking about her farm? But she nodded and said, "It is."

"I asked for directions at the store." He paused as if getting his courage up. Then he asked, "Would Mr. William Spooner be about?"

"Mr. Spooner is dead. He died in the Battle of Saltville in Virginia." Eliza clenched her jaw. What right did this man, this Southerner, have to ask about Will?

"I feared as much, and I am most sorry to hear

that." He removed his cap and bowed his head for a moment before looking Eliza full in the face. His face was as gray as his eyes. "Then you'd be Mrs. Spooner, Mrs. Eliza Spooner."

Eliza gave a single nod, wishing the man would get on with it, then leave. A Southerner asking about Will left a bad taste in her mouth.

"I have traveled from afar to Wabaunsee County to find you, then," he said. "You see, ma'am, I have come to thank you. You saved my life."

CHAPTER ELEVEN

August 18, 1865

Eliza stared at the man as if he had escaped from an asylum. He did not appear demented, but who could tell? If the war had softened the minds of Union soldiers such as the Espy boy, then surely Confederates had been affected, too. Perhaps the man was suffering from soldier's heart, that fatigue that came from seeing too much war. She was a little afraid of him. What he said did not make sense, because she had never met him. How could she have saved his life?

As if he knew what Eliza was thinking, the Confederate gave her a slight smile and said, "You need not fear me, ma'am. I am right in my head, only a little weak for I have walked from Kentucky to this place."

Eliza looked into his sunken eyes. "To see Will?"

"Yes. Or you. I owe you a great debt, you see."

His life, he had said, but Eliza could not imagine how that could be possible. Was it the portion of the harvest she had donated the year before? A government man had come to the farm in late fall and demanded a part of the crop for the soldiers. It was her responsibility to the Union, he'd said. Her husband was fighting in the South, she had told him. Wasn't that sacrifice enough? All the more reason to donate to the cause, the man had said. But the harvest was scant, and they might go hungry. Still, he had insisted it was her duty. So in the end, she had let the man load his wagon with bushels of corn, all the while wondering if the soldiers would see any of it, or whether it would be sold on the black market, with the man pocketing the proceeds.

But how would this Confederate standing in her barnyard know about the corn she had given away, and if he did, why would he come all the way from Kentucky to thank her? The man seemed sincere, however, so she gestured to the stump where she had been sitting. He eased himself onto it, then dropped his bedroll and bread sack next to it. Eliza's scrap bag was open beside him, and he fingered a strip of cloth, a homespun green plaid that was so old it had come with her from Ohio. "You quilt, do you?" Before Eliza could respond, he answered his own question. "Of course you do."

"You did not come to talk of quilting," Eliza said, thinking now that if the man was not suffering from mental distress, he was at least odd. What man talked of quilts?

"In fact, I did," he said, reaching for his bedroll.

He unstrapped it and rolled out a soiled coverlet.

Eliza stared at it, not understanding at first. Then she gasped as she made out the red and white stripes and the triangle of blue with its white stars in the center, although the quilt was so dirty she could barely see the colors. She looked up at the man, her eyes wide, then studied the quilt again, reaching down and touching it with the tip of her finger. It was ripped and tattered, the down gone in some places, spilling out in others. Slowly, she turned over the corner on the lower right-hand side and read the names that were still embroidered there. When she could speak, she said, "This is Will's quilt, the Stars and Stripes quilt I made him for Christmas."

"I did not know it was for Christmas, of course. But I have known all along that you made it for your husband."

"It was for Christmas, last year. He promised to keep it safe."

"It kept me safe. It warmed me in the Rock Island prison camp. I would have died without it."

"But how did you . ." Eliza's voice died at the terrible thought that came to her. She dropped the corner of the quilt she was holding and stared at the soldier. Her legs were weak, and she reached out her hand to steady herself. The soldier jumped up and took her fingers, but Eliza snatched them away. "You," she said. "How did you get it? Will never would have parted with it. You are a Confederate. You are like a dagger in my heart. You must have killed him." She sent him such a look of anguish that the man winced.

"No. Never. I did not." The man rose and held out his hands in supplication.

"Then how else could you have come by his quilt?" Eliza wrung her hands, then stilled them by wrapping them in her apron.

The man gestured to the seat, and it was Eliza who sat down now, steadying herself by grasping the sides of the stump so hard that her hands were white.

"I did not kill him. I never saw him," the man said. "I was captured in a skirmish just before the battle. The Yanks won, and when the fighting was over, we prisoners were marched through the camp. I'd lost my own bedroll, and it was cold, December, so when I saw a quilt nicely rolled up and bound with straps, I snatched it up. I thought someone would take it from me, but no one saw me, so I pretended it was mine. Only after I unrolled the quilt that night did I realize it was a Union flag. I thought it a great joke, and so did my fellows, but it kept me warm."

"It was no joke," Eliza said softly.

"I am sorry. I did not mean to offend."

"You stole my quilt—Will's quilt?"

"Would you rather it had been left on the ground to rot?"

Eliza stiffened. "I would rather it had been Will's shroud."

The soldier sighed. "Ma'am, I am sorry to bring you distress, but there were no shrouds. There wasn't time. The dead were placed in trenches and covered with dirt."

Eliza put her hands over her face, but she did not cry. The soldier touched her shoulder in a gesture of sympathy, but she flung away his hand. "Will wrote me of the graves, but I did not want to believe his remains had been disposed of in such a sacrilegious way, stacked in rows like cordwood in a ditch." Then she muttered to herself, "But why should Will have been any different?"

"I helped to bury the dead. I want you to know I did so with respect."

"Did you bury Will?"

The man shook his head. "How would I know? I felt sorry for the dead. It was only luck and by God's mercy that some of us lived while others died. The Yanks were our enemy in life, but in death, we are all just men."

"You did not act with hate?"

"Oh, I did when the war started, and with good cause. But by the time I was captured, I was too weary of war to hate. I just wanted the killing to stop."

"As did we all," Eliza said.

"I wanted to live."

And so did Will, Eliza thought. She reached

down and traced one of the stars with her finger. The stars had been hard to stitch, because she had tried to make them all alike. It was a pity she had not thought to let them be lopsided and stubby like Missouri Ann's stars.

"Sometimes at night when I lay under the stars on the quilt, I wondered if I would ever again see real stars under a free sky. It was hell, that camp. So many died of smallpox and the bowel complaint, from starvation and the cold. I was there only a winter, but I would have died, too, without your quilt. That's why I had to come here, to return the quilt to Mr. Spooner, to explain why I'd stolen it. That seemed a way I could make peace with the unspeakable, and maybe he could, too."

"You don't hate the Yanks?" Eliza asked.

"Oh, I did at the start, hated them as much as you must hate those of us who fought for the Confederacy. You see, I had a farm in Kentucky, a good one. I had no slaves, didn't believe in one man owning another, so the Southern cause was not mine. Then the Yanks came and burned down the farm. I was away, and Mary, my wife, tried to stop them. She was shot, and I returned home just in time to hold her in my arms as she died. Later I found out a band of Union renegades did that awful deed, but still I blamed all Yankees. If they hadn't started the war, none of this would have happened and Mary would still be with me. I had no reason to stay on, so I joined the

239

army to kill as many Union soldiers as I could. After a time, I was aware the Northerners were much like us—farmers, blacksmiths, shop-keepers. I realized it wasn't the Billy Yanks I hated but war itself and what war did to men."

He paused, then looked down at the quilt. "At the camp in Rock Island, I'd trace your husband's name with my finger, and I knew he wasn't much different from me, with a wife and maybe a farm. I got to pretending that we were friends, that he'd loaned me the quilt. It helped me."

"Your children?"

"They never lived beyond babyhood. I suppose if I'd had someone to go home to, I wouldn't have come here. When the war was over, I went back to Kentucky, but I couldn't abide to on the farm. I left. I'd had many an imaginary talk with Mr. Spooner when I was in prison and had it in my head that I owed him. I even thought about how you'd scold him for losing the quilt you'd made. Mary would have scolded me, although she'd have done it with affection. I thought maybe I'd keep on going west after I returned the quilt."

"War has taken its toll on you, M . . ." Eliza paused. "You did not say your name."

"Judd. Daniel Judd. And it has taken its toll on you, too, Mrs. Spooner, and on your family," he replied. Eliza followed his look around the farm and saw through his eyes the barn whose side was caving in, the fence that was broken in places, the house, where chinking had fallen out. "We shall manage," she said.

"I had expected to find your husband here, had hoped to at any rate. As I tramped the roads, I gave much thought to what I would say to him. As I had no hatred for him, I wished he had none for me. I thought we might have sat as you and I are doing now and talked about the war, although it may be early for such conversations of reconciliation. And I had hoped he was not maimed or his heart hardened by the terrible events."

"I wonder yours was not. After all, you lost the war." Eliza was ashamed at the bit of triumph she felt in saying the words, but she could not help repeating them. "We were the winners."

"I was never a hating man, not until the Yankees burned the farm. And I am not now." He closed his eyes for a moment, then added, "My wife, her last words to me were, 'Don't turn hard, Danny.' I didn't heed them at first, but I try now." He nodded to emphasize his words.

"She must have been a good person."

"The finest I ever knew."

"As was Will. There never was a better man."

The two were still for a moment, each thinking, recalling. Then Daniel smiled at Eliza. "We have both suffered grievous loss." He looked around the farm again. "It appears you need some work done. I could stay a day or so. It is little I can do to repay what I owe."

"No need. I have a son." Eliza wondered what Davy's reaction would be if she asked him to work with a Southerner.

"It might be he could use the help."

"There are men available, Northern men."

Daniel smiled a little, as if to ask, where are they? Then he frowned. "If you're thinking you would have to pay me, I would refuse it. Surely your saving my life is worth a few days' labor."

Eliza was tempted. With Missouri Ann gone, the farm had gotten beyond her, and she needed the help. But she said, "I would not ask it of you."

"I have been on the tramp every day since I left Kentucky. I would welcome a chance to spend two nights in one place. You have a barn with straw where I could sleep, I expect."

Eliza nodded. "You would not be the first to sleep there, although you might be the first Southerner."

"Then it is agreed."

"For just a day or two. I would not want to take advantage of your good nature."

As Eliza and Daniel talked, Davy drove the mule into the barnyard. "His withers are swollen," he said, then stopped when he saw Daniel. But he was used to the soldiers who came by the farm, so he only nodded at the stranger.

"I could take a look. I've worked with mules all my life," Daniel said, straightening up. Eliza observed again how gaunt he was.

Davy exchanged a glance with his mother, and Eliza nodded. "Appreciate it," Davy said.

Daniel went to the mule and ran his hand over its back. "A fistula," he pronounced. "Mules are susceptible. Cold water will take care of it. Add another blanket under the saddle when you ride him."

"Yes, sir. Thank you." Davy held out his hand. "I'm David Spooner."

"Daniel Judd."

The two shook hands, but as they did so, Davy's eyes dropped to the quilt lying on the ground. "Isn't that Papa's quilt?" He looked up at Daniel.

"I'm returning it."

"You knew Papa? You fought with him?" There was excitement in Davy's voice.

"I picked it up near the battlefield."

"You were one of the Kansas Volunteers?"

Daniel glanced at Eliza, then said, "I was a Confederate soldier. I was captured at Saltville."

Davy dropped Daniel's hand and took a step backward. "That's where Papa died. You fought Papa." He turned to his mother. "He killed Papa?"

"He was captured just before the battle," Eliza told him. "He found the quilt lying on the ground and picked it up."

"Is that what he says? How do you know it's true?"

"I believe him. He came all this way to return it." Eliza paused. "He will stay a few days to help us on the farm."

"We don't need help from a Johnnie." Davy stood with his feet apart, defiant.

"We need the help of someone, and Mr. Judd has offered."

"We don't need it from a Yankee-killer," Davy all but yelled.

Eliza put her hand on her son's arm. "Be still, Davy. The war is over. We are one nation again. Mr. Judd has offered to help, and I am grateful for it."

"If you'll take the mule to the barn, I'll bring a bucket of water," Daniel said. "I've a way with mules."

"Just like you've a way with Union soldiers." Davy looked hard at his mother, but she was firm. So Davy led the mule away, while Daniel drew the water. Once her son was gone, Eliza said, "I guess we have accepted your offer of aid, Mr. Judd. Now I must get to supper. It is not much, just hish and hash. We will gather at the table in an hour."

"I'm not fit company for a supper table, Mrs. Spooner. My clothes are more dirt than cloth, and I'm ashamed to tell you I've got graybacks. If you would be kind enough to put a little food on a plate, I will eat it here at the stump."

"We will eat together," Eliza told him. "My

daughter, Luzena, will bring you hot water and soap, and you can wash yourself. You must wash your hair and beard, too, for the creatures like to hide there. I'll find a set of my husband's clothes for you to wear." She looked Daniel up and down, taking in the torn and filthy clothing. "I suggest you burn your own."

Daniel gave her a wisp of a smile. "We call that giving the vermin a parole."

Supper was awkward. Davy was surly, while Luzena was uneasy, sneaking glances at Daniel and turning red when he caught her. Eliza tried to make conversation, but she was afraid she would offend their guest with some question or observation, so she talked in generalities. Daniel seemed to be the only one at ease, asking questions about the farm, about the work that should be done. When the meal was finished, Eliza gave him a quilt, and Daniel went to the barn to bed down.

"Why'd you give him Papa's shirt and pants?" Davy asked.

"His own clothes were rags, and he had lice," Eliza replied. "That's why I sent Luzena with the lye soap and told him to wash well. We wouldn't want to catch the graybacks from him."

"Graybacks," Davy scoffed. He was honing his knife on a whetstone. "Isn't that what the Confederate soldiers with their gray uniforms are called? I guess they're lice, too." He rubbed the knife hard against the stone. "What help will he be? I saw him when he washed. His ribs stick out, and he is as thin as a skeleton."

"He was in the prison camp at Rock Island. It must have been an awful place," Eliza said, scraping the supper scraps into a pail for the chickens. When she came to Daniel's plate, she noticed there was not so much as a drop of gravy left, and she wondered if her chickens ate better than the prisoners had in the camp where Daniel was interned.

"Serves him right. He's a Secesh, and he stole Papa's quilt," Davy said.

"Then he has been punished enough. I imagine that these scraps would have been a feast for him at Rock Island. I have heard it was as foul a place as ever existed."

"Not as bad as Andersonville where the Confederates kept the Union prisoners," Davy said. "They say men fought over rats for supper."

"Ugh!" Luzena said.

"That's not all," Davy began, his voice rising. "They starved our soldiers. Their teeth fell out, and their tongues hung out of their mouths like this." Davy stuck his tongue out of the side of his mouth.

"Enough," Eliza said.

"They were all bad, those prisons," said a voice from the doorway.

The three inside the house whirled around. They had not seen Daniel standing there. He continued, "At Rock Island, smallpox killed two thousand men. They died like sheep with the rot. The food was scarce, and what there was of it was spoiled and odorous. I was so starved I felt my bones were ready to drop out. You say the men at Andersonville ate rats. My best day at Rock Island but one was when I cornered a dog and shared him with two others."

"And the best day?" Luzena asked.

"That was when I walked out of the prison gate, free, and climbed aboard a train for Kentucky. I did not even look back at that awful place. The Confederates did not have the corner on mean prisons."

"The men at Andersonville froze to death. I heard it in town from a soldier who'd been there that the only shelters were shebangs, made from blankets and tarps. At least there were barracks at Rock Island."

"The winters in Illinois are harsher than Georgia's, and fuel was scarce. I myself stood with one foot on the edge of the grave and would have gone up if it hadn't been for the quilt." Daniel glanced around the room for the flag quilt, but fearing it, too, had lice, Eliza had hung it on the clothesline.

"Serves you right. You Johnnies started the war," Davy said, but Eliza told him to be still.

"I did not mean to bring dissent," Daniel told Eliza. "I will leave in the morning if you think it best."

Eliza dipped her hand into the washbasin and took out a plate, a china one. She wondered why she had brought out the good plates for the soldier. "No, I would like you to stay for a day or two, as we agreed. But you must be aware that Davy has lost his father in this war, and he is angry. I would ask you to respect his feelings."

"And he mine?" Daniel asked.

"Yes, that, too, I suppose," Eliza said.

Daniel came into the room and held out his hand to Davy, who ignored it. Daniel only nodded as if he understood and said, "I came to tell you the mule is resting easy. I believe the cold water treatments will work." He turned and left the room.

Eliza and Luzena watched him disappear into the darkness, and Luzena asked, "Are you glad he came, Mama?"

"I don't know," Eliza replied. Indeed, she was conflicted. She could use the man's help on the farm. Still, it might have been better if she had not known what had become of her quilt. She might have continued to believe that Will had been wrapped in it before he was laid in his grave, that he would have rested in it for eternity.

Eliza took another plate from the dishwater and said, "Tomorrow, I shall wash Papa's quilt."

・・・

Eliza scrubbed the Christmas quilt as hard as she could without tearing it further, and when she was finished, the quilt was presentable, if in poor shape. In spare moments, she repaired the rips, although she did not replace the missing quilt pieces nor the duck down in the places where it had escaped. Perhaps she should have burned the quilt, Eliza thought on a hot night as she sat on the porch, the mending in her hands. But she couldn't bring herself to do so. Will had had the quilt only a few days, but he had slept under it. The quilt had warmed him on his last night on earth.

Most men didn't appreciate the creativity of women's hands, but Will was one to notice. He had brought her pins or needles or even pieces of cloth when he went to the store, not much, only a quarter of a yard or so, just enough to cut into shapes for a quilt. Once he returned with a strip of fabric he said was called "Persian Pickle."

"Those little squiggles do indeed look like pickles," Eliza had told him, inspecting the paisley fabric. The material was blue, and Eliza had used a piece of it in the Christmas quilt. She stroked the patch with her hand as she remembered how Will had sat beside her as she sewed, watching her hands as she took her small stitches. Sometimes he helped her with the colors.

"You think you could teach me to quilt?" he asked once.

"You think you could teach me to plow?"

"Done it already."

That was true. Eliza looked at Will's big hands and shook her head. "I don't know how you'd hold a needle," she said.

"I could put together pieces of your material so it'd look like fields," he'd said, and Eliza had grinned at him.

"You could join my quilting circle."

Will had reddened. "I'd never live that down, would I? You'd have to promise you wouldn't tell anybody I helped you."

And so the two had designed a quilt together, a strange one with different-size squares and triangles to represent the crops. Will had gone off to war before the Spooner Farm Quilt, as he called it, was done, and the half-finished top had been put away in the trunk. Eliza had taken it out in the spring, thinking she and Missouri Ann could stitch the remaining pieces in place, but she had started to weep and thrust the top back into the trunk. How long, she had wondered then, how long before every reminder of Will would no longer make her cry? She still cried, she thought now, but not as often.

"I suppose I shall store the Christmas quilt in the trunk," Eliza said one evening as she completed the mending. Daniel had been there two weeks.

"Hang it on the wall," Davy told her. "It's

God's flag." He glanced at Daniel with a look of triumph.

Eliza did not see the look, and said, "I think your papa would like it there." And then she wondered if Daniel would be offended.

He was not. "A good idea," he said.

Davy seemed disappointed he had not gotten a rise out of Daniel and told him, "It's better than the Rebel rag."

That remark offended Daniel, who put down the hames he had been holding, polishing the brass knobs with a rag and a bit of salt, and said, "I will not allow you to profane the flag under which I fought." He spoke quietly, but there was steel in his voice.

"*You* will not *allow?*" Davy retorted. "This is my home, not yours, and it is a Union home. Papa died because of your dirty rag."

"Davy," Eliza spoke up. "Mr. Judd is our guest."

"Mr. Judd is our enemy. You have been taken in and done for, Mama."

Eliza felt conflicted. Davy was right about one thing. This was his home, not Daniel's, but she would not tolerate such disrespect.

Before she could speak, however, Daniel stood. "I would not allow any man to dishonor my flag, just as I would allow no one to do the same to yours. Now I will say good evening, Mrs. Spooner." He rose, the hames in his hand, and left.

"He has overstayed," Davy said. "Why hasn't he gone?"

"You know yourself he has been a great help. We could not have done so much without him. I do not understand why you hate him so, Davy." Eliza picked up the quilt and sat down in the rocking chair, spreading the quilt over her lap. "The fighting is done, and we can't bring Papa back. Mr. Judd is first a man and only second a Confederate. It seems like all your hatred for the war and Papa's death are centered on this one man."

"And don't *you* hate him? Even if he didn't kill Papa, he could have. He's a Secesh." Davy started for the door, saying he would check on the animals, but Eliza told him Daniel would do that.

"You see, he's taken my place," Davy said.

"You mean you complain that he is doing some of your chores." Luzena chuckled.

But Davy would not smile. "Papa would not want him here," he said. "He hated the Secesh. I'm only treating him the way Papa would. Oh, why couldn't Papa be here and that Johnny lying in the grave!"

Later that night, when the children were asleep, Eliza went out onto the porch and sat down on a bench under a dark sky to think about what Davy had said. What *would* Will think about a

Confederate living on the Spooner farm? It was only for a short time, she told herself, not even till harvest, for if Daniel wanted to go west as he had said, he would have to leave before the weather turned cold. It was dangerous for a man alone to cross the Great Plains in winter. As she looked out at the stars, Eliza remembered sitting on the bench not even a year before, finishing the Stars and Stripes quilt and thinking it would keep Will warm. And it had. But it had warmed one of Will's enemies, too.

After a time, Eliza became aware that she was not alone. The Confederate was sitting on the stump between the house and the barn. When had he come out? Perhaps he had been there all along, sitting in solitude as she emerged from the house. Eliza wondered about his thoughts. Were they of his home and his wife, Mary? He had suffered the death of his beloved, just as she had, and the loss of his farm, too. Well, it served him right. He was the Rebel, the one who had started the war. For a moment, Eliza tried to muster Davy's anger, his outrage, any emotion she could against Daniel, but she realized he was just another human being who had suffered greatly. In fact, he had more cause than Will had to fight the war.

"Mr. Judd," she said, and Daniel rose and walked to the porch, where he leaned against a post.

"I've disturbed your reverie," he said.

His words made Eliza realize Daniel was a

learned man. She had thought of him as a farmer, but his speech told her that he had been raised a gentleman. "I am alone too much with my thoughts," she told him. "I would welcome a conversation."

"As would I. What is it you would wish to talk about?"

"Anything but the war." She thought a moment. "Tell me of your boyhood."

Daniel sat down at the edge of the porch, his back to Eliza. "I saw a broken rocker beside the barn. I'll repair it for you, and you can use it on the porch instead of a bench."

"I would like that," Eliza said, thinking he did not want to talk about himself. She had been bold in asking it.

But after a pause, Daniel said, "It was the best growing-up time a boy could have. My father was a banker, and we lived in a fine house. I had four sisters, and they doted on me. Father taught me to ride and hunt and fish, and when he was not working, we would disappear into the country-side, just the two of us. He sent me to the university, intending that I become a banker, but I loved the outdoors too much, so he set me up on a farm."

"He is yet living?" Eliza asked.

"He died before the war began. I am grateful for it. The devastation would have brought him anguish."

"And your sisters?"

"They are all right, but we had become estranged."

"They were for the North?" Eliza asked. She knew that the war had torn apart families with divided loyalties.

"No," Daniel said, and was silent. Eliza thought once again that she had been too forward. She said nothing, and at last, Daniel told her, "They did not care for Mary. You see, she came from a poor family and was unschooled. My sisters thought I had married beneath myself. They had it in mind I would connect with one of the better families, and by doing so, assure our place in society. But our hearts make the decision of whom we love. Mary was smart as a whip, and I myself taught her to read and write."

Daniel stared out into the darkness, and neither he nor Eliza spoke for a long time. Eliza thought she had pried too much and did not want to cause the man further anguish. But at last, she said, "I, too, have been guilty of thinking with my heart. I believe it is not such a bad thing."

"You did so when you took me in."

Eliza was embarrassed at Daniel's reply and was glad it was too dark for him to see her blush. The conversation had become too familiar, and she stood and said she must go inside. She took a step toward the door, but Daniel said, "Mrs. Spooner," and she stopped. She did not turn around and waited for him to continue. She heard him rise and take a step toward her.

"I do not want to cause trouble in your family. I will move on if you think it best. I had believed your son would accept me, since we seem to work side by side in harmony. But I know he resents me and blames me for the war."

"Do you want to go? You said at the outset that you expected to go on west." Eliza felt a sudden chill, and she shivered. She wished she had put on her shawl. But it was not the cold that made her shiver.

"I do not wish it at all. I was of poor heart when I came here, and I believe the work has made me better. I would like to stay through harvest, if that has your approval. I am as good a hand with a scythe as any farmer, and if there is a machine about that can thresh the wheat, then I believe we could hire it."

"I have no money for such a machine," Eliza told him.

"I expect to have a little coming in. I would like to spend it to pay you back for your hospitality."

"It is I who owe you for work on the farm. It is poor pay to receive only a straw bed in the barn and your supper."

Daniel put his hand on Eliza's arm, and she felt the warmth of it through her sleeve, felt her blood warm at his touch. Something inside her stirred, and frightened, she pulled her arm away.

"It would not be proper for me to accept your aid," she said.

Daniel dropped his hand, and took a step backward. "Forgive me, Mrs. Spooner. Being around a family has made me forget my place."

Eliza wanted to tell him he had not offended her, but something made her stop. "Yes," she muttered and went inside and closed the door.

In the fall, Daniel moved into the soddy. The weather had turned chill, and while Daniel said the straw in the barn was warmer than the bed he'd slept on at Rock Island, Eliza knew he would be better off in a house. She and Luzena scrubbed the one room and washed the muslin that they had stretched across the ceiling after Missouri Ann and Nance moved in. The cloth was there to catch the dirt that fell from the sod roof. Eliza added fresh straw to the tick. Although he grumbled, Davy repaired the table and chairs that the Starks had broken in their frenzy to find the escaped slave girl. Daniel patched the sides of the building where the sod had come loose. When they were finished and Daniel had arranged his few belongings in the house, he pronounced it as comfortable a home as he had ever had.

"Don't get too used to it. You won't be here for long," Davy told him.

CHAPTER TWELVE

October 13, 1865

Eliza's quilt group knew right off that the Confederate hired man had moved into the soddy. When they met at Eliza's farm the October day not long after Daniel left the barn for the little house, they saw him emerge from it and nod to them, although he was not forward enough to approach the women. They nodded stiffly in return, then exchanged glances behind his back.

"He's living there then, the Secesh." Eliza had gone into the house for her scissors, and Anna whispered.

"Botheration. It's enough to knock you down," Ettie said.

"Is he a rogue, do you think?" Anna inquired, leaning forward, her voice low. "They're all rogues, all the Confederates. I reckon he's eating white bread now, living here on Eliza's farm, in that little house, dining at the supper table."

"Oh, yes. For him, the goose hangs high," agreed Ettie.

"We all know she's needing a man bad to help

with the work. Davy's a boy yet," Mercy told them, defending Eliza's decision to let the Rebel stay. "I can understand it."

"She'd have no need of him if she could find a husband," Anna told them.

"And where would that be?" Ettie asked. "I've not seen a surplus of men around here, what with so many gone up in the war. They say there's a whole generation of Southern women who are destined to be widows and spinsters, and the Union's lost a plenty of its own, too."

Mercy looked out over the farm, at the leaves that were just starting to turn yellow. "Will Spooner was her heart's soul."

The quilt group was smaller now without Missouri Ann, and the three women were setting up the frame on the porch for fear of rain. Eliza, inside, overheard them. Mercy was right; she did need a man on the farm. Of all the quilters, she was now the only one who would work the land alone. Missouri Ann had married, Anna's and Ettie's husbands had come home, and Mercy was betrothed to John Hamlin. They had announced their intention to marry after the harvest. Already one of John's hired men was helping with Mercy's farm.

She was amused and a little disappointed that her friends were talking behind her back, but she held her head high, pretending she hadn't heard, and stepped out onto the porch.

"God bless me, we were gossiping about you just now," Ettie admitted, as the women arranged chairs around the quilt frame. "We were saying as how that hired man of yours moved into the soddy. Looks like he'll stay a while."

"Just until the harvest is done," Eliza told them. "It didn't seem right to make him sleep in the barn, what with cold weather coming on, when there's a perfectly good house he can use." She helped the others set in the quilt, white with flower baskets appliquéd to it. The top was Mercy's work and was intended to be one of her wedding quilts. "Mr. Judd's a worker," she added by way of compliment.

"You expect he'll leave then, your hired man?" Ettie asked.

"He's not exactly a hired man, because I'm not paying him wages. He says the work brings back his sanity, poor fellow," Eliza told her.

"Maybe if we hard-worked all the Secesh, it'd bring them back to sanity," Ettie said, with more than a trace of sarcasm in her voice. She had turned bitter after her son returned, his soul heavy with war. "Not that they ever had any to start out with."

"Rubbish, Ettie. We ought to move on. The war's over and done with." Anna sat down and threaded her needle.

Ettie gave her a hard look. "Not for some of us, some that's lost one son and got another at home with soldier's heart. The trials my poor boy had

260

were enough to make a good Christian cuss. I could pray till the crack of doom, but I can't find forgiveness in my heart for the South. It's a wonder, them killing your husband, you'd even speak to a Confederate, Eliza."

Eliza had begun quilting, but she stopped and waited until Ettie looked up at her. "He's not a Confederate anymore, Ettie. He's just a man."

"They're always Confederates," Ettie retorted.

"Is that the way Davy feels?" Mercy asked. She had begun stitching around one of the flowers on her quilt. Her work had improved greatly, and Eliza marveled at the cunning stitches.

"No," Eliza said at last. "Davy can't forget who Mr. Judd is. Sometimes I feel like I have a chained bear in the house with me."

"Then why do you keep the fellow on?" Anna asked.

"Because we need him. And because I feel safer with a man about." Eliza did not add that Daniel eased her loneliness.

Ettie worked at a knot in her thread with her needle, then gave up and tried to yank the knot through the fabric. The thread broke, and she muttered, "God bless me. I'm always a-doing this. I'm as useless as a half-pair of scissors." She put the length of thread attached to the quilt into her needle and added, "I have no one to thank but myself, the way I'm carrying on. I wouldn't want a Rebel living so close to me, but I got men at home to help out. It's your doing, Eliza, and I'll rest my mouth about it."

"We all will," Mercy told them, looking up at Eliza. "Have you heard from Missouri Ann? Is there a baby yet?"

"Just the one letter, and the baby isn't due until the new year," Eliza answered, and the women, glad to have the discussion of the Confederate behind them, turned to lighter subjects.

But Eliza brooded and did not join the conversation. The others, even Ettie for all her talk, had put the war behind her. Only Eliza seemed to be standing still, not knowing what lay ahead. She caught sight of Daniel in the distance as he walked to the well and took a dipperful of water from the bucket. He did not glance her way, but Eliza stared at him, wondering how she would cope after he moved on. And he would leave, she knew, even if he wanted to stay, even if *she* wanted him to stay. He and Davy had come to a sort of truce, but that would end with the harvest. It would be better when he was gone. The harvest would be a good one, and perhaps she could hire a man—a Union man—to help with the planting. In time, Davy might soften toward his father's enemies, but he wouldn't now, not when one of them slept on their farm.

She returned to her quilting, her eyes on a red

tulip in Mercy's quilt, unaware that her friends had been watching her as she watched Daniel.

One day in November, Daniel returned from town with the news that he had found a threshing crew and at a good price.

"It can't be much of crew if that's all they're charging," Davy said.

"Men need work," Daniel replied. "They take what they can get."

"Are they Secesh?" Davy asked. He was helping Eliza pick the last of the tomatoes in the kitchen garden.

"I didn't inquire their pedigree," Daniel replied to Davy's question. "I know only that they were sturdy men, and their equipment is in good condition. As they were already in the county and looking for more work, they gave me a good price. They will be here on Monday."

"You had no right to hire them. How will we pay for them?" Davy asked, yanking at a tomato so hard that he crushed it and the juice spilled over his hand.

"I believe we have that much to spend," Eliza put in. "A crew at that fee will pay for itself, for it will harvest everything in the fields, far more than the three of us could do. I thank you, Mr. Judd."

"I'll oversee them and make sure they do a good job," Daniel promised.

"*I* will oversee them. This is my farm," Davy told him, rubbing his tomato-stained hands on his pants.

Eliza glanced at Daniel to see if he was offended, but he didn't appear to be and, in fact, replied, "Of course, Davy."

After the boy left to take the dishpan of tomatoes into the house, Daniel told Eliza, "He resents me yet. I had thought our working together would soften him."

"As did I. You have worked well with each other. Perhaps his feelings toward the Rebels will change in time."

"Not before I leave."

"You are going, then." Eliza yanked out a denuded tomato vine so that she did not have to look at Daniel.

"That was the plan. Is there a reason to change it?"

There was no reason, Eliza thought, except that she had grown used to having him around. The farm now ran almost as well as it had before the war, when Will was in charge. But it wasn't just the farm. Eliza enjoyed having a man to converse with, to discuss politics and events at the supper table, and to talk about softer things on the porch at night, after Davy and Luzena had gone to bed. Sometimes Daniel recited the words of poets she'd never heard of, or talked of his joy in raising horses. Once as he looked out toward the fields that he could not see in the darkness, he told Eliza how satisfied he was seeing her land prosper under his hands—his and Davy's, he added quickly. It was the sort of conversation she would have had with Will. She would be lonely without this man.

Still, Daniel was a Rebel, one of their enemies, and it would be easier for Davy after Daniel left. She thought about Will. Would he have wanted the Johnnie to stay? What would Will have thought about a Confederate living on the farm, working the fields *he* had broken, using the tools *he* had crafted, living in the soddy *he* had built? The thought that Will would not have approved troubled Eliza. This was Will's farm. It always would be. So, for that reason alone, it was best that Daniel move on. "No, no reason to change," Eliza answered his question.

Daniel reached for the tomato plant Eliza held, and their hands met. Eliza was shaken by the touch and withdrew her hand, dropping the plant. Daniel stared at her for a moment, then reached for the vine.

"I must be at supper," Eliza said, although it was only early afternoon, and Luzena did the cooking now.

Daniel nodded, not glancing away. When Eliza reached the porch and looked back, Daniel was still staring at her.

They skipped church on Sunday so that Eliza and Luzena could start on the pies and bread, the chicken and potatoes and all the other food the threshing crew would expect. Eliza wanted to prepare as much ahead of time as possible. Now the bounty of food lay on the table—a feast really, for nobody ate as much as threshers. Eliza was tired from the day's work and the anticipation of more the next day, but when the pans and dishes had been put away and Luzena and Davy were upstairs in the loft, Eliza went outside on the porch to cool herself. Perhaps one day she would have a cook stove, but for now, the cooking was done in the fireplace, and her shoulders ached from lifting the heavy pots. The fire made her feel scorched.

She sat down in the rocker that Will had made and Daniel had repaired and wiped her face with her apron. Her dress was damp with perspiration, and her hair had slipped out of its knot and curled in the heat. She saw then that Daniel was standing in front of the soddy, and when Eliza glanced his way, Daniel, unbidden, walked slowly to the porch. Was he the reason she had come outside? No, she told herself. It was foolishness to think such. She would stay only a minute, then go to bed, for she must be ready when the crew arrived.

"It will be a hard time, the next days," Daniel said. "You had best get some rest, Mrs. Spooner."

"And you. You yourself will be working with the threshers."

Daniel lowered himself to the porch. "I've always liked that kind of work. You don't brood as much when you're working."

"You brood, then."

"No more than any other. I believe you do so, too."

Eliza did not respond to the remark, but asked, "Will you look for a farm in the west?"

Daniel shrugged in the moonlight. "I haven't decided. Perhaps I can find a gold mine then buy myself a ranch, one right here in Kansas. I never saw such a big sky as here. Or land that begs to be plowed. It would be a good place to settle."

She did not tell him she liked that idea. Instead, she remarked, "Print Ritter, our blacksmith, went to Colorado to find gold and thought he might return to buy a farm. But I am afraid there may be more gold seekers than mines."

Daniel laughed, and Eliza liked the sound of it. "Would you go west, Mrs. Spooner?" he asked.

What did he mean by that? Eliza wondered, then decided he was just making conversation. "It was our intention, Will's and mine, but we liked Kansas too well. Will thought the land the best he had ever seen for farming," she replied. "I thought it a good place to raise a family. I could see my grandchildren living here one day."

Daniel glanced up at a sound in the chicken

coop and rose partway, but the noise stopped, and he sat back down. "What was he like, your Will?" he asked. Eliza paused as she thought over her answer, paused so long that Daniel said, "I am too forward. I'll say good night."

Eliza held out her hand to stop him, but his back was to her. "No, I am not offended. I was trying to think how best to describe him." She thought for a moment and began. "He was a steady man, slow to anger, but once aroused, he would not back down. He was a good man, and neighborly. There wasn't anybody who asked for help who didn't get it from Will. He worked as hard as you do, Mr. Judd, and you know what a fine farm this is. But mostly, I think of him as a good husband and father. You have seen for yourself how Davy mourns him."

"Do *you* blame me for his death?" Daniel's voice was low, and there was a catch in it.

"No more than you blame Will for the death of your Mary."

Daniel nodded, his back still to Eliza. "Funny, isn't it, how we fought each other for four years, and now we commiserate. We're not much different, Northerners and Southerners. We're husbands and wives and children, farmers, merchants, preachers." He chuckled. "Preachers on the North and South, and each one saying as how God was on their side."

"Maybe half of them were right," Eliza said.

"You think he favored the North?"

"It might be said He was against slavery." She thought a moment and added, "But no, I do not believe God takes sides. I believe He must have detested the war and wished we could have gotten along."

"That's a God I'd like."

Eliza pondered Daniel's words and said, "You haven't come to church with us, Mr. Judd. Do you not believe in God?"

"Oh, I believe. But perhaps I do not believe I'd find him in a Yankee church." He stood and turned to Eliza. "I am only jesting, Mrs. Spooner. I know your friends and neighbors do not approve of my being here, and I do not want to cause trouble for you."

"It is trouble I would bear, Mr. Judd."

The threshing went well. The weather was fine, and the crew was efficient. Daniel and Davy worked almost as one, never arguing or disagreeing, Eliza observed. They made a good team, understanding without having to talk about each task. It was the way Davy had worked with Will. Despite Davy's claim that he was in charge, he and Daniel managed the threshers together. Eliza was pleased. Perhaps Davy was more accepting now, more forgiving of the Confederate. That would be good for both men.

The harvest, then, was a good one, better than

Eliza had expected, and she thought perhaps their years of hardship were over.

And then on the last day of threshing, Davy stumbled on a rock in the field and fell in front of the threshing machine. The machine caught his arm and twisted it under him, and with a scream, Davy curled into a ball, senseless. Daniel turned in time to see the accident, and he scooped up the boy, running with him to the house. Sweat poured down Daniel's face and arms, and he was gasping for breath by the time he reached the barnyard. "Mrs. Spooner," he yelled, but Eliza had gone out into the stubble of the field and did not hear him. He rang the dinner bell, then carried Davy into the house and laid the boy on Eliza's bed. Two of the threshing crew had followed and stood in the doorway not sure what to do.

"Build up the fire. Heat water," Daniel ordered, as he ripped off Davy's shirt to examine the arm. It was bloody and bruised, and bones penetrated the skin. Daniel moved the arm to make sure it was still in its socket, and Davy moaned. "Steady, boy," Daniel muttered.

As Daniel straightened the arm, Eliza rushed into the room. "I heard the bell. Is it one of the threshers?" she asked, as she hurried to the bed. Then she blanched and put her hands to her mouth. "Oh, dear God, it's Davy. How bad is he hurt?"

"Plenty bad. It's his arm. It's broke in two places. He needs a doctor."

"The one we have is an old sawbones and a drunk. I'd almost rather set the bones myself."

"You know about such things?" Daniel asked.

Eliza shook her head. "Do you?"

"I've cared for dogs and horses, set their bones. I guess it's not so different." Daniel wiped his forehead with his sleeve. "But they don't feel the pain like Davy will. Do you have any whiskey?"

Eliza thought, then shook her head. The Starks had taken the last of it.

One of the threshers stepped forward and took a pint bottle from his overalls. He held it out.

Daniel nodded his thanks, then told the man, "Hitch up Mrs. Spooner's buggy and fetch the doctor. Even drunk as a pigeon, he'll know more than I do."

The doctor's office was next to the general store, with a sign reading DR. FISH, Eliza said.

The thresher nodded and hurried out.

Eliza moved to heat water, but the second thresher, having already built up the fire, was pouring water into an iron teakettle. He hung it on a crane, which he pushed over the fire.

"See if you can get the whiskey in him," Daniel said. "He'll need it when I set the bones."

Eliza nodded and lifted her son's head, pouring the whiskey into his mouth. Half of the liquid spilled, but some went down the boy's throat, too, and Davy coughed, then began moaning again.

"I need hot water and soap," Daniel said. The

271

thresher poured water from the kettle into a basin and brought it to Daniel. Eliza fetched the soap. "Might as well start with clean hands," Daniel told them.

Eliza found cloths and used one to wipe Daniel's face. With the fire built up, the room was hot, almost stifling, and Daniel had been running.

He glanced up at Eliza and took a deep breath, then he slowly straightened Davy's arm and began pushing at the bones. "I'll need strips of cloth for bandages and a stick to hold the bones in place," he said. Eliza began tearing the cloths, while the thresher ran to the kindling pile for a stick. Daniel told him to pour boiling water over, for it might have dirt or bugs.

Davy groaned, and once he sat up and cried out. The boy was delirious, Daniel told Eliza, as she pushed her son back down on the bed. He had seen such delirium at Rock Island. Daniel gritted his teeth, then slipped the bones into place. He took a deep breath, and still holding the arm, he slid a cloth under it. "I would not want to soil your quilt," Daniel said.

"The quilt be damned!" Eliza told him, not even shocked by words she had never thought to utter, especially at the ruination of her favorite quilt, the Rain and Sunshine quilt that had been her wedding present to Will.

The two worked together quietly, Daniel wrapping the arm while Eliza handed him the bandages and then the stick. They were finished by the time the thresher returned with the doctor.

Eliza was surprised to see them so soon and remarked on it. "Oh, I didn't take your buggy. There was a mule out there, and I jumped on him. He acted like he'd never been rid hard before," the thresher told her.

"He hasn't," Eliza said.

"Well, he has now."

The doctor went to the bed and asked, "What seems to be the trouble with this young man? Malingering at harvesttime, is he?"

"My son has broken his arm, and Mr. Judd set it," Eliza replied stiffly.

"A doctor, are you?" Dr. Fish asked.

"No," Daniel replied.

Dr. Fish examined the arm, turning it back and forth, making Davy cry out. "Well, you might as well be. Good as if I done it myself. Ought to have a sling, though."

"Will he be all right?" Eliza asked.

The doctor shrugged. "I imagine he'll have use of the arm. It's bringing down the fever you got to worry about. Put out the damn fire so it don't get too hot in here. Give the boy water and put cold cloths on his head." He glanced at the pint bottle on the table, picked it up, and took a swallow. "I wouldn't be giving him too much of this unless it's for the pain. Alcohol ain't good for a fever." He started to put the bottle into his pocket, but the thresher stepped forward and claimed it. "Oh, my mistake," the doctor said.

Daniel walked Dr. Fish out the door, then returned, Luzena a few steps behind him. She had been taking water to the threshers and had not heard the bell. Until she saw the doctor's horse, she hadn't known anything was wrong.

Eliza held out her arms to her daughter, who rushed into them. "Davy's broken his arm," she said, hoping Luzena would not catch the worry in her voice.

"And Dr. Fish set it."

"Mr. Judd did."

"Then why did he pay the doctor?" Luzena asked.

Daniel finished up with the threshing crew, then saw to the animals. While Daniel was milking, the head of the crew came into the house, removed his hat, and inquired about Davy.

"He's well as might be expected, thanks to Mr. Judd and two of your men who came to help."

"Little enough we could do."

"I must pay you for the threshing," Eliza said, going to the pie safe where she kept her money.

"Oh, your husband already done it," the man said. "I just come to check on the boy."

"He paid you?"

The man nodded, while Eliza wondered when Daniel had gotten the money. He must have seen her put it into the pie safe and taken it out. But when she opened the door of the cupboard she saw that her money was still there.

"We sure would like to do your threshing next year," the man said, and smiled. "And I won't charge extra for staying on like I done this time. In fact, if I'd knowed what a worker your husband was, I'd have bid a lower price."

"He is my hired man," Eliza corrected, and then she wondered what he meant by "charge extra." "Exactly how much did he pay you?"

The man gave a figure that was half again what Daniel had told her the work would cost.

"I see," Eliza said, frowning, although she didn't see. Why had Daniel committed her to such a high price?

"About next year . . ."

She would wait until she found out how good the next year's crop was, Eliza said.

Daniel offered to take the first watch with Davy that night, but Eliza told him she would sit with her son. She knew Daniel would be tired from his work with the threshing crew, as well as caring for Davy. She could see he was exhausted.

"I'll sleep a little while, then relieve you," he said, and left the house.

Eliza lit a candle and pulled a chair close to the bed. Luzena called down from the loft, "Mama, do you want me to sit with Davy while you rest?"

Eliza told her to go to sleep, that she'd sit and read her Bible. She smoothed the quilt over the boy, a fresh quilt. Luzena had removed the soiled one and soaked it in cold salt water. But that had not removed the stain, so in the morning, Eliza would rub it with cornstarch. She did not worry much about the quilt, however. After all, quilts were made to be used up, even those such as the Rain and Sunshine that had been made for special occasions. Instead, she dipped a cloth into a basin of water on the floor beside her and wiped Davy's brow. He stirred but did not awaken. She studied her son's face in the candlelight, noting that it was no longer the face of a boy but of a young man. She smiled to see how Davy had grown a mustache so pale and slight that she had not noticed it before, and remembered Will at that age, half boy, half man.

She intended to read her Bible, but she thought of Will's letters and decided to read one of them instead—one of the last he had written. So she removed it from the candle box and sat down next to the fire, holding the paper in the firelight.

December 7, 1864
Dear Wife
This will be short. We marched in the rain past Rebel graves washed clean of dirt so that I saw the hands of the dead sticking out as if

beseeching me to pray for them. We will rest in the mud for an hour, then march on. I write so that I do not fall asleep, for if I do, I will not wake until doomsday. Tired, very tired. My bones ache & I have a little fever. Bullets were flying thick yesterday & we have not slept in more than two days. May God watch over me this time of terrible war.

The order is given to move on. I send my love & wish it would warm you as your quilt does me.

Your Husband
William T. Spooner

Eliza returned the letter to the candle box and sat down next to Davy, her head on the bed. She had intended to rest only a little, but she fell asleep and did not wake until she felt a hand touch her arm. She sat up suddenly, thinking Davy had need of her, but it was Daniel's hand that had awakened her. "I did not mean to startle you," he said.

"What's the hour?"

"Not yet dawn."

Eliza stood up quickly and examined Davy. The boy's breathing was ragged but he slept. She reached for the cloth to wipe his forehead, but his face was damp, and Daniel said he had washed the boy's face.

"While I slept?"

"No need to wake you. I only just came in. I thought you might like to go up to the loft and lie down. Your back will hurt from sleeping the way you did."

But Eliza was awake and said she would sit a bit longer so as not to disturb Luzena. "That is, unless you're wanting to eat." In the turmoil of the day before, they had not had supper.

Daniel shook his head. He carried a chair to the other side of the bed and sat down on it, then reached across the quilt and took Eliza's hand. They stayed like that until dawn showed through the window, and Eliza rose to prepare break-fast.

The three of them—Eliza, Daniel, and Luzena—did Davy's chores, then took turns sitting beside the boy. With the threshing done, there was not so much work now. Eliza's friends heard of the accident and came with beef tea and custard for Davy, soup and pie for the others. The women insisted on sitting with Davy while Eliza went outside for air.

"Sick begets sick," Ettie told Eliza, shooing her out for a walk in the orchard. The weather was cold, but the brisk air felt good after the sickroom, and the fallen apples smelled like cider. Eliza returned refreshed, and left the door open to cool the room. Davy had been in and out of consciousness, but when Eliza turned to the bed, she saw his eyes were open. "He woke just after you left," Ettie said.

Eliza rushed to the bed and put her cold hand against Davy's face. His forehead was no longer hot. "The fever is gone," she said, and would have hugged her son, but he had closed his eyes again, and Eliza supposed he had gone back to sleep.

As Eliza gazed at Davy, Daniel entered the room. "Almost good as new," Ettie told him. "The boy'll be out milking again before you know it." Daniel glanced at Eliza, and they exchanged a look that caused Ettie to stand and collect her things and say she must be on her way.

Later that evening, as the two sat on the porch, bundled up against the cold, Eliza told Daniel that Davy might have died without him. "I believe if you hadn't stayed for harvest, Davy could be dead. You saved his life, Mr. Judd."

"You put too fine a point on it. If I hadn't stayed for harvest, there wouldn't have been a threshing crew, and Davy wouldn't have been hurt at all."

"There's that." Eliza laughed, feeling light-hearted because of Davy's recovery. But then she frowned and said, "There is something between us that needs clearing up." She took a deep breath. "I must pay you for the threshing crew."

Daniel relaxed. "Oh, that. Yes, if you must."

"I mean I must pay the full price. You had no right to commit me to such an amount."

"I didn't."

"The price was more by half than what you told me."

Daniel shifted his feet and looked at the ground. "We needed threshers, and I had the money. It came to me a month ago from the sale of my farm."

"I cannot accept it. I will pay you the balance after the money for the wheat comes in."

"I won't take it."

"You have no choice," Eliza told him.

Daniel, who had been sitting on the porch step, rose and stood over Eliza. "You saved my life. Do you not think my life is worth that small amount of money?"

"I cannot accept it." Eliza would not budge. "You saved Davy's life, so that cleans the slate. Besides, you have worked for us without compensation these last months. It is I who should pay you."

"I am not so poor as you think," Daniel told her. "I sold the land in Kentucky for a good price, as well as the horses. I can afford to pay your threshers. And you will suffer from privation next year if you don't let me help you."

"That is not the point, Mr. Judd."

"But it is precisely the point, Mrs. Spooner."

Eliza shook her head and said she would have

the money for him before he moved on. "You will be moving on, of course." Then she added, "Won't you?"

"I don't want to. Perhaps I should stay a little longer, until Davy is well. You'll need help with his chores."

Eliza felt a weight lift from her heart. For a moment, she did not trust herself to speak. Then she said in a steady voice, "And leave at Christmas then? Or the spring?"

"Or maybe never."

Eliza stopped rocking as she mulled over the words. Daniel put his hand on her shoulder, and she glanced down at his fingers, slender but strong. "I might have need of a hired man next year," she said.

"I am not talking about being your hired hand."

Eliza was rigid now, staring out at the leaves that blew across the barnyard. Then she pulled her shawl around her, her finger poking through the thin fabric. "This is not a proper conversation."

"It is entirely proper, for my intention is honorable. I came here to return your quilt, and when I saw the condition of your farm, I stayed on to help. It was the least I could do. But I fell in love with you, maybe even on that first day. I thought it best to leave after a week, but I couldn't. Perhaps I should have, because I did not believe you would return the affection of a

Confederate. But I have come to hope otherwise. After all, we are no longer North and South but united now. I would like to stay on and farm this place with you—as your husband. Will you accept me?"

Eliza stared straight ahead, not at Daniel but at a leaf that had blown against the porch. It held for a moment, then another gust of wind lifted it into the air and swirled it away. Her mind, like the leaf, was in turmoil. Did she love this man? She had never thought to marry again, had never examined her feelings toward him. But over the last weeks, she had grown comfortable with him, had not wanted him to leave.

"Mrs. Spooner?" Daniel said. "Eliza?"

"I don't know, Mr. Judd. I don't know what to say. I can't think."

He knelt beside the rocker. "But you will think about it. Tell me you will."

Eliza nodded. "I will. I will think about it." Daniel rose and started to turn away, but Eliza took his sleeve. "I must wait until Davy is better, but I will think about it."

CHAPTER THIRTEEN

November 20, 1865

Eliza slept little that night. Her mind wandered from joy that Davy's fever was gone and worry about whether he could use his arm, to confusion over Daniel's proposal. Before dawn, she awoke and quietly built up the fire. Then she ground coffee, mixed it with water in a pot, and set the pot in the coals. While the coffee boiled, she moved silently to Davy's bed to see if he was awake. But he slept soundly, so when the coffee was thick and black, she poured it into a tin cup and went outside to watch for the dawn.

While Daniel's proposal had shocked her, Eliza realized now that she should have expected it. He had been leading up to it, perhaps for weeks. Of course, she should have made clear she was not interested in marrying again, asked him to leave before the harvest or to go off with the threshing crew. Marrying a Confederate was out of the question. Davy would not stand for it. Her neighbors would not. How could she marry a man who had fought against the Union, against her husband? Besides, Will had not been dead a year. What would people think of her marrying again so soon? And then she smiled, remembering how pleased she'd been when both Missouri Ann and Mercy had found new husbands so quickly.

Eliza had been leaning against the porch post, the cup warming her hands, and now she lowered herself to the step where Daniel usually sat. She watched a bird land in the barnyard and peck at something in the dirt, then fly away. She had considered how others would respond, but what about herself? Could she love a Southerner? Did she love him already? She hugged her knees, for it was cold, and she had gone outside without her shawl. Yes, she thought at last. Yes, she did care for him, and in time perhaps, she could care for him as much as she had Will. Theirs could be a good life together, maybe even as happy a one as she had had before. She and Daniel were more alike than different. Both of them loved the earth and the things that grew in it. They had already worked together in harmony. They'd shared laughter and joy, and both had had sadness and loss. Yes, it could be a good marriage, Eliza thought, if only Davy would accept it. Luzena would, but Davy . . . she wasn't sure.

She sipped at her coffee, turning to look at the soddy and through the window saw a match flare, and then a candle flicker. Daniel was awake. Eliza did not want him to see her on the porch.

He might think she was waiting for him. So she rose and entered the house, going about the business of making breakfast. As she took salt pork from the larder and mixed batter for flapjacks, Eliza heard Davy stir and then call to her softly. Eliza set down the bowl and went to her son, smoothing the quilt. "You are conscious at last." She could hear the gladness in her voice.

"I feel as if I've slept a week."

"And so you have."

Davy grimaced as he moved in the bed, then looked down at his arm. "I remember the thresher knocking me to the ground, but after that . . ." He looked at her, bewildered.

"You broke your arm in two places. You'll have to be careful, wear it in a sling until it heals." She felt his head, but the fever had not returned. "Mr. Judd picked you up and carried you back to the house. He set the bones."

"Mr. Judd?"

Eliza nodded.

Davy thought that over but didn't say anything. He was looking at his arm when Daniel knocked on the door, then entered. "You are awake then," Daniel observed.

"You set my arm," Davy said. He dipped his head at Daniel in acknowledgment. Eliza wished he would say more, would thank Daniel, but it was a start.

As soon as he was out of bed, Davy resumed chores that could be done with one hand. He had to be careful of the broken arm, Daniel told him. If he tried to use it, he might jar the bones, and they would have to be reset, which would be as painful as the original break. So Davy let the others do much of his work. In the evenings, he and Daniel talked about chores for the next day, about the things that needed doing before winter set in. Davy did what he could, but most of the work fell on Daniel. "Will you stay until I'm healed?" Davy asked Daniel.

Eliza heard the request and smiled to herself. She was sorry Davy had broken his arm, but the accident had drawn the two men together. Davy seemed to resent Daniel less now, and he'd stopped making remarks about Rebels. He had even asked Daniel to stay on. Perhaps he would approve of her marrying Daniel after all.

"I'll stay as long as I'm needed—or wanted," Daniel replied, and Eliza turned away, her face flushed.

Eliza and Daniel did not speak again about marriage. Then one afternoon in December, as she was feeding the chickens from a basin tucked under one arm, she saw Daniel put the hay fork aside and come toward her. She turned away as she scattered scraps, calling, "Here, chick, chick,

286

chick." The chickens flocked to her as she spread the feed. She ignored Daniel beside her until he told her the basin was empty and took it from her.

"Davy is well," he said, "well enough for me to leave." He set the basin on the ground.

"Is that your intent?" For a moment, Eliza wondered if Daniel's proposal had been a fleeting impulse. Perhaps he hadn't meant it at all and this was his way of telling her.

"You know it is not. But I believe this thing between us should be settled. I will not stay on if your answer is no."

Eliza sat down on the stile and looked out over the farm, at the stubble in the fields that shone gold in the early winter light. There was frost now and perhaps snow in a day or two. Already the weather had turned cold, and she shivered with only her mended shawl to keep her warm.

"You're cold," Daniel said, touching her arm. "I should like to buy you a warmer shawl."

"That would not be proper."

"It would be if I were your husband."

Eliza smiled at him. "Yes, you are right. Do you think I would marry you for a new shawl?"

He grinned back at her. "It's as good a reason as any and better than some."

"Would it be a paisley shawl, a red one from Scotland? I have always wanted one."

"Two if you like. A dozen."

"And how would we pay for seed for spring planting?" Suddenly, Eliza felt lighthearted. She remembered how she and Will had teased each other, had laughed together at their silliness.

"We would find a way," Daniel said. He put his foot on the stile and leaned over her.

"I believe you could," she said. After all, he had found a way with Davy. "Then I will say yes to your proposal, Mr. Judd."

"I had rather you say, 'Yes to your proposal, Danny,' " he told her. He raised her until she stood close to him, and Eliza thought he would have kissed her if they had not been standing in the barnyard in plain view of Luzena.

That night after supper, Eliza told the children she had something to announce. She glanced at Daniel, then reached across the table and took his hand. "Mr. Judd and I are to be married."

Davy and Luzena looked from Eliza to Daniel, and back at Eliza. Luzena's mouth dropped open, and then she grinned. "Mama, that's fine. Just fine," she said.

Eliza turned to Davy then, hoping he had been so easily won over. But her son stared at her, his face strained, and it seemed to Eliza that he was not breathing. She was holding her breath, too, Eliza realized, and so was Daniel. "Davy," Eliza said at last.

Suddenly, Davy's fist came down on the table,

hitting it so hard that milk spilled out of the pitcher. "I won't have it," he said.

Shocked, Eliza stared at him. "*You* won't have it?"

"I won't let you, Mama. He's a Rebel. He fought against Papa. You know how Papa hated the Confederates. You would dishonor him."

"But you know Mr. Judd. He isn't a soldier anymore," Eliza said. "We could not have gotten along this fall without him. You work with him as though the two of you were a team in harness. I thought you had put your hatred behind you."

"He's not so bad as he was. I'll give you that. But he's a *Southerner.* You can't marry him, Mama. You would shame us. Papa hated Johnnies. He'd hate you, too, if you married one."

Eliza, embarrassed to be holding Daniel's hand, released it and put her hands into her lap. The joy she had felt that afternoon was gone. "Your papa is dead, Davy. We have to go on."

"Not with *him.* He can stay on as a hired man, but if you marry him, I'm leaving." Davy rose from the table so suddenly that he knocked his chair to the floor. "I got milking to do."

"You can't milk with one hand," Daniel said, rising. "I'll do it."

"Don't need help from a Reb." Davy clomped out. Snow had begun to fall, and cold air rushed into the room before Davy could slam the door.

Eliza slumped in her chair, while Luzena rose and began clearing dishes.

"I'll speak to him in the morning after he settles down. He's got no right to talk to you like that," Daniel said.

"No, he's my son. I'll speak to him. He's come this far toward you, Daniel. Perhaps he won't be so hard tomorrow."

"And if he is?" Daniel asked.

Eliza shrugged. "We'll see."

Davy did not soften. In the days ahead, he refused to speak to Daniel, refused to let Daniel help with his chores, and Eliza worried that Davy would reinjure his arm as he struggled to assert himself. She talked to him. She had the right to marry, she said. Davy nodded in agreement, then told her he wouldn't oppose her marrying a Union man. Daniel had saved Davy's arm and maybe his life, she argued. Then the two men were even, Davy insisted, because she had saved Daniel's life with the quilt. The war was over. It was best to move ahead. But when Eliza told Davy that, he remained firm. How could they move ahead with a Johnnie in the house? His presence would remind them every day that the Confederates had killed Will. "I will never change my mind, Mama. Marry him, and I will leave the next day. I hate him, just as Papa hated the Rebels."

A little more than a week later, Daniel followed

Eliza into the barn and said they must talk. She seated herself in the undertaker's sleigh and looked up at him in the dim light. The day was dark, and snow had begun to fall.

"We can't go on forever like this. It tears at me, and you, too, I think. I do not believe Davy will change toward me," Daniel said.

"No."

"Then you have a choice to make."

"Davy's my son."

"And nearly a grown man. He may leave you one day whether you marry or not."

Eliza ran her hand over the words embalmers of the dead written on the side of the sleigh. She had never gotten around to painting them out. "This is the only home he's ever known. How can I make him leave?"

"Then you've made your choice."

"Have I?" Eliza looked up at Daniel. "I don't want to choose."

"Then I will. I love you, Eliza, but a marriage between us would have no chance if your son is opposed to it. I think we could have had a good life together, but that seems impossible now. It's best I leave."

"Leave?" Eliza stood and brushed straw off her apron. "When?"

"Now. Tomorrow, today even."

"So soon?" Eliza felt tears in her eyes. "Couldn't you wait? You could be here until spring. If Davy hasn't changed his mind by then . . ."

"And leave my heart out there to be stepped on? No. If it's not to be, then I'll go now." He reached into the sleigh, took her hands in his and pulled her toward him, then kissed her. "I have loved you," he said.

"And I you."

Daniel looked at her a long time. Then without another word, he left the sleigh and went out into the snow, the barn door swinging shut behind him. Eliza stared at it a long time, stared at the light that came through the cracks between the boards. Then she wrapped her tattered shawl around herself and went out into the storm. She felt the snowflakes sting her face as the wind swirled the snow around her. Maybe the storm would keep Daniel there one more day, she thought as she went inside the house to help Luzena prepare the evening meal.

Supper was as strained as it had been on Daniel's first days on the farm. Luzena chattered, but Davy refused to speak, while Daniel and Eliza tried without much luck to keep a conversation going. The meal was conducted in silence, punctuated only by the wind blowing against the house.

"The snow should stop by morning," Luzena said.

Daniel and Eliza looked at each other, but were

silent, and Luzena, not understanding, ceased talking. As soon as supper was finished, Daniel rose, saying he had things to do before going to bed. "I'll check the chickens and the animals," he told Davy.

"Suit yourself," Davy replied.

Daniel did not look at Eliza as he rose, but when he opened the door, he turned to her and she saw a look of longing on his face. Was that same look on hers?

After the door closed, Davy looked up and said, "Riddance."

"Be still," Eliza told him.

The next day, Daniel was gone. He left no note. In fact, there was no trace of him at all in the soddy. Eliza wasn't sure when he had left, but she knew it was after the snow stopped, because she could see his tracks, which went from the soddy to the barn and then down the lane.

"Most likely he took the mule," Davy said, when Eliza told him that Daniel had moved on.

"He was only checking the animals a last time. He is an honorable man—just like your father," Eliza told him. She said she would do the milking and went out to the barn herself, thinking Daniel might have left some word of farewell for her there. The mule and the cow and the horse had been fed. Daniel had forked fresh straw into the stalls. The tools hung from the wall in rows where he had left them. Eliza glanced around and took in the work Daniel had done. He had repaired the buggy top, replaced the seat on the wagon, rebuilt the manger. This was Will's barn, but Daniel had left his mark on it. She placed the stool behind the cow and began milking, watching the warm liquid stream into the pail, thinking that only the night before Daniel had sat on that stool, milking the cow.

In a little while, Davy came into the barn and said, "I can do the milking now, Mama."

"You'll hurt your arm. I'll do it until you're mended."

"We don't need that old Secesh. You'll see. We can manage just fine. I'm glad he's gone. Think of Papa. Remember how he hated the Rebs."

Eliza did not respond. She had a great desire to be alone, to lie down in the hay and cover herself with it. But in time, she picked up the pail and went out into the gray of morning.

When she returned to the house, Eliza took out her piecing. Sewing had always soothed her, so she removed the square that Clara had left and laid it on the table. She had been holding it when she first saw Daniel, and she had not picked it up since. She had thought then to use it as the center of a quilt and surround it with squares and triangles. Now, Eliza took scraps out of her bag and laid them around the quilt to see which colors went best with the square. But she could not concentrate, and the house oppressed her, so despite the cold, Eliza went back outside. She fed the chickens and broke the ice in the water trough. She went into the barn, climbed the ladder to the hayloft, and pushed hay down onto the barn floor. Then she stood at the haymow door, looking out across the white fields, looking in the direction Daniel had taken. But he had left hours earlier, and there was no sign of him. She stood there while her hands and feet grew cold, and her face was red from the wind and the blowing snow.

In a little while, Davy came out of the house, and Eliza watched him as he looked around, at the fields, the chicken coop, then hurried toward the barn. He did not see Eliza standing in the open doorway in the loft until he was halfway there, and then he held up a paper and shouted something, but his words were lost in the wind. Perhaps Daniel had left a note after all, maybe in the soddy, but what did it matter? He was gone.

Eliza did not leave her place. She stayed in the doorway, still staring out at the white fields, while Davy climbed the ladder, then came up next to her. "Look, Mama," he said. She glanced down at the paper in his hand, a letter. Daniel had indeed written something to her, but she did not care.

"The letter," Davy said.

"Yes," Eliza replied, but did not take it. Instead, she reached for a piece of hay and shredded it. What could Daniel write that they hadn't already said to each other?

"It's Papa's letter."

"What?" Eliza's head jerked up, and she felt tears come into her eyes.

"His last letter, the one Papa wrote just before he died."

Eliza looked at the letter that Davy had unfolded. "You read it? You read your father's last letter? How dare you, Davy! It was mine. I never intended to open it. I could not bear to read his words, knowing he died only hours, maybe even minutes after he wrote them. How could he have known he'd die that day?"

"But he did," Davy said. "He knew. Read it, Mama."

Eliza snatched the letter from her son and clutched it to her breast. "No, I couldn't."

"Please, Mama."

Eliza closed her eyes and shook her head.

"You have to."

Eliza looked down at the writing. In the gloom of the barn she could not make out the words. She turned toward the light, and holding on to the door frame, she held up the paper. But there were tears in her eyes, and the words were blurry. "Read it to me then if you must," she said.

Eliza thought she saw Davy's eyes glisten, too,

but the light was dim, and perhaps she was wrong. Davy took the letter and cleared his throat.

December 19, 1864
Beloved Wife
They say we will do battle tomorrow & I cannot sleep. No, I do not fear the fight. At first, I worried that I would not be up to the mark & would turn coward. But I believe I have proved myself in the past weeks.

Davy looked up at Eliza, who said, "I had no such doubt. He was always a brave man."

I have got so I can sleep pretty well any-place, but tonight is different. Sometimes the soldiers have a premonition that they will die, so spend the night before the fighting writing their last letters. I myself have not felt that way before, but tonight is different & so I sit by the campfire writing to you.
Eliza, if I die, they will tell you it was for a noble cause, that I was happy to make the sacrifice. Do not believe them. I do not want to die for any reason & I no longer believe in this cause. In the beginning, I thought that ours was a God-ordained undertaking, one that was worth my life, if it came to that. I believed there were things worth more than life & peace. But now that I have seen war &

the suffering it brings, I am not so sure of myself. Those of us fighting are just men who want to go home & I believe now that the Johnnies are no different from us & perhaps more honorable, because they are fighting for their homes. One thing I know is that war is not noble. When I joined up, I hated all Southerners, hated them for a long time & wished you & Davy & Luzena to hate them, too. But now I know that hate is wrong. It is not God's way. It is forgiveness we need. I want the Johnnies to forgive me for invading their land, as I forgive them for fighting against the Union.

Davy stopped and looked up at his mother, but Eliza was staring out at the snow.

Two days ago, after we camped, I went into the woods, believing I had spotted a black walnut tree & thinking the nuts would be a treat, for I remember your candy made with the nutmeats. I took my gun with me, because I knew the enemy was about. So when I heard a noise, I raised my gun & turned & there was a Rebel, holding his gun on me.

"Hello, Billy Yank," he said & I replied, "Hello, Johnnie Reb."

"Well, I guess I have got you," he told me & I told him back, "And I have got you."

We stood like that for a time, our guns pointed at each other, until the Reb said, "I propose we call a truce & have us a confab." Before I could answer, he put down his gun & grinned at me.

Eliza blinked back tears. "I can just picture him," she said.

Now, Eliza, I could have laid him aside right there, shot him through the heart & some would say it was my duty to do it, but I am not made that way. It would not have been right. So I set aside my gun & we squatted down & talked.

"This is better land for a farm than a battle," he told me.

"Any place is better for farming than fighting," I said.

"You got that right, Yank."

Why, we sat there & talked for a good half hour. He was just an uneducated sandlapper & I doubt he could read or write, but he was a good fellow & he took out an apple, shined it on his pants & we shared it. He showed me his wife's picture & I showed him yours. After a while, we shook hands & wished each other good luck. I suppose I should have held my gun on him & backed away for fear he would use me up, but I trusted him. It bothers at me now that I might face him on the battlefield tomorrow & have to kill him. I do not want to ever kill a man again. Now, you will say I have soldier's heart & perhaps I do. But I want to be done with killing as I am with hating & I want you to be done with hating, too.

If I fall in the battle tomorrow, I do not want you to live out your days with abomination in your heart. Don't, don't be sad, Eliza. Remember me as a husband who loved you as much as my life, but do not live the rest of yours like a bird without a mate.

It is nearly dawn & there are other camp-fires now & soon there will be furious drumming, so I must end. I hope you never see this letter, for if you do, it will mean that I am no longer with you. But if you receive it—when you receive it—know that I love you deeply & that I count our time together as blessed. I am sorry only that we will not live out our years together. And that I never bought you a gold ring with a ruby in it.

Davy's voice was ragged, and tears streamed down his face—and Eliza's—now. "Is that all?" she asked when he did not continue.

"Only a little more."

Davy is nearly a man now. Keep him from this war. I do not want him to know the

300

hardness that comes of it. Raise up our children to be worthy of you & I would like to think worthy of me, too. My final wish if I do not return is that you put aside grief & find happiness.

God help me now.

Your Loving Husband

William T. Spooner

Davy folded the letter so that it was as an envelope again and held it out to Eliza, who took a step away from the haymow door and reached for it, holding it in her cold fingers. "I should have read it before," she said. "What made you open it?"

Davy shifted, rubbing the toe of his foot on the floor and scattering hay. Then without looking at Eliza, he said, "I thought Papa had written something that would make you glad Mr. Judd left."

"But he didn't."

Davy shrugged. "It's my fault he's gone." He said in a raw voice, "I think Papa would have wanted him to stay."

"It's a pity we didn't read his letter before. Things might have turned out differently." She touched the letter to her cheek.

"They still can."

"What do you mean?" Eliza asked.

"I was wrong." Davy glanced at Eliza, then

stared past her to the barnyard. He seemed to struggle with himself. "Papa told you to be happy. He said not to hate."

"But you still do?"

"I don't know. I don't want to now." Davy turned away from his mother and slammed the fist of his good arm against a support. "Damn!" he said, hitting the post again. Then he shook out his arm to get rid of the sting. "Do you love him, Mama, Mr. Judd?"

She nodded.

"As much as Papa?"

Eliza shrugged. "I'll never know. But I believe he is as good a man as Papa."

Davy stared at her for a long time. Then he hurried down the ladder.

"What are you doing?" Eliza called.

"He can't have got so far, walking that way. I'll fetch him. Me and the mule will make good time, better than with the buggy." Davy picked up a saddle blanket and fitted it on the mule's back, doubling over the back of it so the saddle would rest higher, just as Daniel had told him that first day on the farm. Using his good arm, he swung the saddle over the mule, and in a moment, he led the animal out of the barn. "I'll be back," he called. "Me and Mr. Judd will be back."

EPILOGUE

December 24, 1865

Eliza and Daniel were married on Christmas Eve, Davy and Luzena standing up with them. The weather had been good and the roads dry that day, so the members of Eliza's quilting group and their families had come for the ceremony, bringing a cake the size of a washbasin. The three women had made it together, each contributing to the ingredients. Mercy brought the flower-basket quilt as a present from all of them.

The gold ring Daniel slid onto Eliza's finger did not have a ruby in it but a blue stone, a sapphire "the color of your eyes," Daniel told her. They looked at each other as they said their vows, Eliza wearing the new paisley shawl Daniel had given her, then turned to John Hamlin, who officiated, as he asked a final blessing.

Just before she bowed her head Eliza glanced at the quilt hanging on the wall in front of them, the Stars and Stripes quilt she had made just a year before. The white stripes were dingy and the red ones faded, but the blue was still bright, and the white stars stood out as if they were hung in the sky. Eliza gave thanks that it had kept Will safe for a time and had saved Daniel's life. And now, she knew, the ragged quilt would warm their lives for all the Christmases to come.